WORK

LOVE

BALANCE

The Story of ADAM

© 2013 Samer Chidiac

Copyright © 2013 Samer Chidiac
Published by ChidiacBooks.com

ISBN-13: 978-9953021409

"I've learned so much from you; your love & care gave me motivation to be the best of what I can be..."

To my lovely sister
Yusser Chidiac

The Story of Adam

The events and characters in this book are inspired by true events and real life personas.

It All Started with...

Misconceptions of Life & Love

"You go to school, you study hard, you find a Job, you climb the ladder, you make good money and you find Happiness"

~The Father

"You should fall in love, get married and live with the one that makes you happy... Now remember The ONE is out there, you need to look very carefully, and when you do, you need to constantly buy her flowers, take her out to eat and cuddle her and shower her with   Gifts"

~The Mother

Those were the first theories Adam was raised on, at a young age his parents didn't teach him much; His father taught him about work from his own experience but practically most of the learning came from Adam watching his father working hard most of his time and coming late to the house to complain about everything from Boss to Salary to everything.

And While the Work learning came from the father, the learning about Love came from Adam's mother, she loved him so much, and always protected him and gave the warmth of motherhood to his life... but her theories on Love was based on her own experience and on drama she watched on TV. (Adam's mother married at a young age, Adam's father was the first and only man in her life whom she met and married when they were studying in college).

Throughout his young years at school, Adam was not particularly an A student nor an F, and his life with the Ladies was more imaginary than real.

Fast forwarding through his College life, he faced lots of financial difficulties that had him working his way of paying the tuitions... and on the personal scale he gone through the exercise of casual dating and he always was the nice guy like his Mother taught him.

Whatever most of us have been through in school and college, Adam's experience was almost similar; his girlfriend then was not a cheerleader, his part-time jobs were more hands than brains and paid minimum wage... He had fun nevertheless, studied hard and got a Bachelor degree after all.

After College; Everything out of sudden became... REAL!

Finding a job was not as easy as he was taught in college (Get a degree and Doors will be open for you wherever you go); Adam had to start from less than Zero.

As tough as it was for Adam to get a job and Start Climbing the Ladder, keeping his job was a bigger challenge... His personal life was also heading from one failure to the other... Apparently being Nice was not good enough these days.

Depressed he was; Adam was working long hours to pay his bills, he had an average social life, maybe because he had good friends which made his life worth living.

One evening as he was heading to his night shift at a 24h supermarket, he heard the voice of an old man screaming from the alley: "HELP... HELP... PLEASE HELP ME..."

Adam Rushed to see what's going on, he saw a 70 years old man who fell of his wheelchair and a bunch of young boys trying to take his merchandise; he quickly ran toward them and as soon as he arrived the boys ran away and left the old man shaking from fear.

Adam: "Are you OK Sir?"

Old man: "Of course I am... I normally enjoy being on the floor, especially when I can't feel my legs..."

Adam: "Oh I'm sorry; Let me help you out..."

Adam helped the old man getting back on his wheelchair and walked him to his house; Adam was quite shocked to see that the old man lived in an enormous house in the best area in the city close to where his night shift takes place.

Both arrived, and were welcomed by the butler who was very concerned and said: "Mr. Kays, why do you keep sneaking on me and go alone to buy stuff? You got us all worried about you..."

"I got bored... Sue me!" said the old man.

Mr. Kays: "Why don't you make me and my new friend here a nice cup of tea... by the way I didn't catch your name son?"

Adam: "I'm Adam... and thank you very much for the invitation, but I really have to go to my work now... I'm already in trouble for being late"

Mr. Kays: "Very well then... Tomorrow at 7:15 AM we'll have breakfast at my place and I won't take 'NO' for an answer... You'll have enough time to

brush your teeth and go to your day-
Job"

And before Adam has the chance to
say anything, Mr. Kays went inside the
house.

First things first

Breakfast at the Kays

At exactly 7:15 AM the next day, Adam was ringing the Bell of Mr. Kays' house; the door was opened by a woman in her 60s, still looking very charming and with a warm smile she said: "You must be Adam... I'm Mrs. Kays... Please come in."

Adam was astonished while walking through the reception of the big house, everything was wisely placed around and the Kays looks as if they have great taste in Art and Culture.

Mr. Kays was waiting at the Dining room; he smiled when he spotted Adam.

"I would've stand up to greet you... but you were 3 minutes late..." said the old man ironically.

"Good morning to you too Mr. Kays" said Adam.

Mr. Kays: "You can call me Eric... Please take a seat"

All three of them had a delicious Mediterranean breakfast, followed by TEA.

Mrs. Kays: "So Adam... how do you spend your time?"

Adam: "I work at ABC Consulting during the day... and at the Supermarket around the Corner at night"

Mrs. Kays: "ABC Consulting is a Fine firm... You must be one of their talented Consultants... They do employ the Best"

Adam: "Actually I'm in the Archive department... I'm responsible for Data Entry and documents scanning"

Mrs. Kays: "You don't look like a data entry guy... I bet Mickey didn't do his homework when he interviewed you..."

Adam: "Mickey?"

Mrs. Kays: "Michael Moor, VP of Operations; He was one of my interns when I was CEO of Blackwell Inc."

Adam was shocked as he looked at Mrs. Kays, since he was always used to hearing the Man in the family talking about Business stuff... and Mrs. Kays looked like she know her stuff really well!

Mr. Kays interrupted: "Well Samantha that was like 30 years ago, I bet when he will hears your name he would fire the poor Adam"

"Tell me Adam, I bet a good looking guy like you is not getting enough of dating in this city" continued Mr. Kays in an attempt to change to subject to something that would give Adam more advantage.

"Of course sir, I can't keep the ladies off me in this city" Said Adam while smiling nervously...

"Well son, what I started to like about you... is that you're a Terrible Liar" Mr. Kays Said while sipping his Tea.

Adam was shocked and before he opens his mouth to talk, Mrs. Kays said:

"Don't let Eric get onto your nerves Adam, he has a PHD in Psychology with emphasize on Relationships and what you kids call these days... LOVE"

Mr. & Mrs. Kays were certainly very different from any old couple Adam has ever met...

Mr. Kays: "I would like to sit more with you Adam; unfortunately we didn't have any Kids so it would be nice to have you drop by for visits from time to time... I'm certain we would have some set of skills that would strike some useful conversation with you. And I'm sure Mrs. Kays will be delighted to give you some hints on how to progress in your Career..."

Adam was very excited to the idea, thanked the Kays for their hospitality and promised to pass by every Friday after Work to have a cup of TEA and benefit from their long experience in topics Related to Work & Love.

The Golden Advice

Know what you want

Friday came quickly; Adam finished his paper work and went straight to the Kays.

Eric and Samantha welcomed Adam and invited him in; the young 25 years old Adam was shy and humble, he sat and didn't say a word and was barely making eye contact with anyone.

"Long week at the office... how does it feel?" asked Samantha

Adam: "Well you know... cool stuff... things here and there... I'm getting along with everyone pretty good"

Samantha: "Tell me Adam... if I were to ask you what your ideal job is, what would you say?"

Adam: "A good company... Good position... Large pay Check..."

"And how do you plan on getting there from where you are now?" asked Eric.

"I'm very ambitious Mr. Kays, ABC Consulting is a much respected firm and I'm planning on climbing the ladder and step by Step, several years from now, I can be one of their consultants and who knows maybe an assistant manager or so."

"Do you dream of being an Assistant manager at ABC Consulting 10 years from now" asked Samantha while maintaining a direct Eye contact with Adam.

"I Wouldn't Say DREAM... but frankly I'm being realistic" said Adam.

Samantha: "I'll Rephrase my question then... What would you say your Dream Job would be Adam?"

Adam: "I dream to become the CEO of a Major Corporation"

"Now we're talking..." Smiled Samantha

Eric: "What about the Future Mrs. Adam?"

Adam: "Well you know what they say sir, a guy needs to look for THE ONE... The one who will love and care for you and with whom you would be truly happy"

Eric: "Interesting... Tell me more about 'The One' "

Adam: "I don't know... but I'm sure she will have everything I ask for in a girl"

Samantha: "and what do you ask for in a girl?"

Adam: "ummmm.... Well she needs to be Cool... and cares about the Stuff that I like... And have great things..."

Eric and Samantha both smiled mysteriously; then Eric Winked at Samantha to go and do something.

Eric said to Adam: "I didn't have the Chance to thank you the other day, so me and Mrs. Kays got you a small gift of appreciation".

Samantha brought a nicely packaged "notebook" and gave it to Adam.

Adam was delighted to receive a gift from the Kays and asked why a "Notebook" in particular?

Samantha Replied: "This would serve as a good way to write down the experiences we will share with you; and to add your own to them and maybe to share it with someone special in your life"

page 27

Adam smiled big time and started taking notes from the great talk they had that evening.

When Adam was back Home, his mind was full of images and stories that he couldn't fall asleep... he opened his gift and started reading...

"Golden Advice:

You're always on the Look... Everything you do, everywhere you go is an opportunity to Learn, to meet new people (potential clients, the girl of your dreams...)

Now there's the Fact; There's no ONE Right Girl for you, NO ONE Right job for you... there are several Ones that you would be very happy to be with or work at...

the Catch is knowing what are you searching for!

Let's say I told a girl that her charming prince is a tall blond guy with muscles, wearing a Tuxedo and driving a Brand new Mercedes... Now the Minute she will find a guy that fits that profile... BINGO!

IF I told a guy that the perfect Job is working for Microsoft... the guy won't be looking for a Job anymore... he will be looking for a JOB AT MICROSOFT because that's the perfect JOB!

Dr. K said: One of the Things that fascinated me in my life is how people like to (by nature) to be told what to do... What to like, what to hate, how to Live, how to Love...

Mrs. K added...

That's why you find that the most successful people everyone commonly knows are the ones that defied everybody's thought of them and their ideas, and who lived a Life that is considered as different before they became Rich and Famous.

Let me give you a good example (Dr. K):

What is the Measure or Benchmark of Beauty for kids these days? You will find that the Pretty, Tall and Blond BARBIE is it... so if a girl had long legs, blond hair and fancy body, she's automatically "Gorgeous"... because she looks like a Barbie.

And here's another example:

If I told you to visualize a Successful Businessman; I would guess that the first picture that you will draw in your head would be the Wall Street Stock broker wearing his Armani suit, holding a Mobile phone and his briefcase and walking down some large stairs... Right?

Bill Gates is one of the most Rich & Successful people I've heard of, and he dresses like a NERD...

So The Advice is:

Simply don't go with the Flow in measuring and putting stereotypes to people... Learn how people think, Experience what they truly are and then make your own standard that you think is comfortable for you!

Because what you don't like makes sense to someone else.... And the other way around!

So going back to the first thought:

Knowing what you want & what you're really looking for... is KEY... and is where you need to start... And YES it's not as EASY!

Q from me: I have been trying to do so from long time... I don't know how to start... any hints?

Mrs. K: Lots of times you don't know what you want... or what you like... but in 90% of the times you certainly know what you DON'T LIKE... and in this case you need to be HONEST with yourself..

Dr. K: Same thing goes in dating... I still remember my first Girlfriend, and I laugh hard now on how I thought she was the ONE but I had to experience several others... until I found my Samantha. And trust me my Standard matured over the years because back then my standard was based on what I THOUGHT I Wanted!

Mr. & Mrs. K Agreeing: Another key element is Being READY... to meet your Potential Client, your Future Love... You may be waiting all of your life for a specific opportunity and when it hits you in the face you're not ready for it... maybe not looking your best, not having a business card... etc.

Rising up

First day of the rest of your Life

Adam woke up the second day feeling like he was Born again, he was dreaming of what he heard, what he wrote what he Felt after his visit to the K's.

The first thing he did, was to dress up to go to work, although he normally walk unnoticed until he reach his day job, his first surprise was hearing a female voice saying: "Well Hello There..." the 25 years old average looking Adam turned to that voice and saw a 40 something lady smiling at him while continuing her walk.

It felt weird at a start, but for some reason Adam felt that he was the center of the world; he Walked high, looked up and one can see Confidence surrounding him like an Aura.

He reached to his workplace, walked into the office and looked directly in the eyes of everyone, stopped and said while smiling: "Bonjour!" (*Good morning in French*).

Adam definitely made an impression... Sadly, it lasted only few minutes before he was back to his desk with the bunch of files from all over...

That evening, Adam was hanging out with his friends at a fast food restaurant; Valerie and Casa known him since college, and Bach, Nour and MIKE from even before that time;

The gang talked about practically everything... Valerie has always had issues with her Boyfriend, MIKE

Always complained from not finding the right Job, Casa & Nour hated each other's publicly but deep inside everyone knew they had something going between them.... Finally Bach was on another planet, he adored sports to the extent that you would think he was born with a ball in his head instead of a Brain.

Those people where the part that made Adam's life worth living... he loved his friends so much that he would've done anything for each and every one at any time.

"So Adam, how's Work?" asked Nour

"SSDD..." Replied Adam

"Relax Buddy... at least you got one" Said MIKE with sarcasm

Valerie: "Work is Work... la laa laa la laaaa"

And everyone started laughing and continued singing the classic "Life is Life" song...

Well Almost everyone; Bach was a little bit distracted from the group so everyone calmed down a bit and Casa Asked Him:

"What's wrong Bach? You look like you've just saw Michael Jordan quitting Basketball"

The athletic good looking Bach turned and looks at Casa and replied:

"Nothing important really... I just had some stuff I need to decide on... That's it"

"Anything we can help you out in?" Said Adam

Bach: "Have you guys ever wonder what it would be like to live your dreams? Well my dream is to play professional soccer, but everyone I talk to especially my parents thinks this is non-sense and that I need to focus on getting a job in a respected company and forget about sports."

MIKE: "They are right, sports is not made for us, you should forget about it, get employed in a big shot firm and start making good money"

Adam looked at MIKE and said to him in a loud tune:

"Well at least Bach has a dream and he knows exactly what he want and he's Ready to pursue his dream immediately... unlike some people I know... " maintaining eye contacts with MIKE.

Adam continues talking to Bach saying: "You know something Bach, you're very passionate about sports, and if you believe deep inside that this is what you want to do for the rest of your life... Then Do it... Your parents want what's best for you, but apparently you need to do more efforts to convince them to see things from your eyes..."

"Everyone looks at the Taylor profession as being middle to lower Class and they fail to see that Famous fashion designers are also Taylors, Designers that sell 1 Dress for 100,000s of $ while a reputed Banker makes less than 70k a YEAR" said Nour while smiling at Adam as a confirmation to what he was talking about.

Bach felt much better and was very proud to be among his best friends in the whole world.

Valerie was looking at the window of the restaurant when she suddenly freeze as if she has seen a Ghost!

Her boyfriend Charley was holding another girl on the street facing the group of friends.

Charley and Valerie were not the best couple you could think of, Charley was the BAD Boy type and Valerie was a calm respected and smart girl.

Valerie started crying... and everyone started trying to make her feel little better.

"I don't know what you see in this Jerk..." Said MIKE

Casa: "He's not around for you like EVER... he treats you bad and yet you keep coming back to him..."

Adam: "Guys Guys... I think the best thing to do right now is to walk Valerie home, and make sure she's ok... I'll do that, you guys stay here and we'll talk later on".

Adam walked with Valerie to her home and on their way they started chatting...

Valerie: "it's all my fault, I should've been more careful when I chose the man I wanted to be with..."

"No it was not your fault... we sometimes get driven by what we think we want as some things are not for us to control... we can chose whom we can marry but we can't choose whom to get attracted to.. Because Attraction isn't a choice... " said Adam while looking at the trees surrounding the neighborhood where Valerie lives.

Adam continued: "you know Valerie, in life you don't get what you want... you get what you negotiate... especially in your personal life... so if a guy was looking for a SUPER GOOD looking Girl, he would find one... but she may not be the type that he would take her to see his parents... if he was looking for an Super Educated girl, he would find her... but he shouldn't expect that her PHD would compensate her average look...."

"And you my friend, were simply the victim of your ego; you wanted to have the hot guy that other girls wanted, the bad guy who treats you bad but you keep the faith that he would eventually change, just because you believe that you deserve a better life..." Adam finished his conversation when they reached the stairs of Valerie's house.

Valerie: "Wow Adam, I'm so impressed by your words... and even the things you told Bach when we were in the Restaurant... Your words are very mature and very deep... I just wonder why don't you simply APPLY them to your own life and have a better one!"

Adam stood in shock watching Valerie go into her building and he could see a Big Stage SPOTLIGHT pointing just on him and no one was applauding;

He started walking home; his head down with quick steps and on his way he kept thinking about what Valerie said to him... He knew deep inside that she was right, he didn't practice what he preached, never had; But Why? Why does Adam's Advices work like a Charm on everyone else and he can't even apply them on his own life...?

As Adam was walking fast, his footsteps were sounding as a Cinema Film Roll... Suddenly lots of memories were flashing left and right beside him. His life on the left side and his friends' life on the right... Their success through applying Adam's advice and his failure by not applying his.

And while Adam's imagination was in its climax during his fast walk, he remembered a quote from the Classic Movie: "The Godfather"... "It's not Personal... it's Business" and there it Hit Him!

He reached to his notebook and started writing...

The Word Bad is Nice

The Bad Boy Symptom

One day at the office, Adam was doing business as usual, chatting with his colleagues, smiling and laughing as if he had the most important JOB in the world;

10:30 AM, suddenly everything changed, smiles disappear... tension started spreading in the atmosphere, and there comes Joe... The Head of the Department and Adam's Boss.

Joe was a typical stereotype of a Boss, thick glasses, always frowning, never smiles and always observing left and right looking for reasons to start a fight.

"You arrived late today... I wonder what would happen if your paycheck came late this month" Joe looked at Jessica through the room....

Jessica was an excellent employee, she treats her work as a matter of Life and Death and is always willing to go the extra mile, but somehow Joe never appreciated her;

Adam – who get to work late like every other day – got upset, he knew that Jessica must have a good reason to validate her late arrival but he didn't say any word.

Joe was not afraid of showing his dedication to his duties on the expenses of other employees. He continued passing from one employee to the other and giving remarks to each, and when he reached to Adam, he looked him in the eye and said...

"You my friend seem to know someone who knows someone from the 34th floor; if you think you're going to get away from me easily... you're mistaken... I'm watching you... CLOSELY"

Adam was shocked... He had no idea that the building even had a 34th floor at the first place; he kept starring at Joe's eyes without even one comment.

Time flew by till 5 PM; such a weird day for Adam, who still couldn't get over what happened with Joe, he slowly walked to his second Job at the Supermarket.

There's much difference when you work in front of a computer all day, entering data and working with numbers, and then work in a supermarket helping customers find the right merchandise.

The First couple of hours felt so long, customers are much alike at this time of the night but one customer was more familiar than the others... He would recognize her grey hair and sharp look anywhere... Mrs. K!

Adam went over to say hi to Samantha, and offered his service.

Samantha: "Well Hello Young Man!"

Adam: "Good evening Mrs. Kays; it's good to see you"

Samantha: "It's good to see you too... Judging from your uniform, I can tell that this is the 2nd job that you told me about."

"Guilty as charged ☺... I work night shift here 5 times a week" replied Adam

"So you do work in ABC Consulting at day and at a Supermarket at Night... no wonder you arrive late to work sometimes." Said Samantha while smiling mysteriously.

Adam was confused, was it a Wild Guess?

Samantha: "I was having Coffee in ABC Consulting the other day, and was discussing couple of stuff with Philippe, the President & COO there... I gave him an example of undercover talents and mentioned your name... and of course he never heard of you... so he had to call someone to ask about you... Joe Something..."

"So it was you!!" Adam said,

Samantha: "don't get very excited, Philippe now remembers you as the undercover talent that arrives late to work... it's pretty much as flagging you with 'NICE' guy"

"I'm sorry I didn't get the 'Nice' part?" asked Adam.

Samantha: "Nice people in a company normally are those who work to stay on the safe side, they follow the rules, dedicate themselves to their work and to the company.

Nice people play a vital role in the world of corporates, but unfortunately very few of them get where they want."

"Nice people are known that they are the opposite of Tough, they are emotional, they're the ones who play by the rules, and have jobs that are not very critical in the company... Jobs that doesn't require... BALLS..." continued Samantha.

Adam: "Are you saying that I'm looking at a Dead end in my career?"

"I didn't say that..." Said Samantha "but Nice Employees are often the ones that executive meet in the elevators and say: "So you're from Data Entry..." and when they leave to their floor he continue saying "How Sweet...." As if he's looking at a 6 years old who just drew his first painting..."

Adam: "But Mrs. K, isn't NICE something good? And we all should be good in life and in Work?"

Samantha: "Good.... Yes; Nice... Not very often... I'll tell you what, why don't we talk about this more when you come over tomorrow?"

Adam walked Samantha to the Cashier and thanked her for the talk and wished her a good evening.

The Second day, Almost past as if it was on Fast Forward... Adam didn't know how he finished his work to find himself walking toward the Kays'.

Mr. K greeted the young man: "Adam, it's good to see you!"

A small general chit chat between Adam and Eric took place that felt almost as if Eric was talking to a Robot that was programmed to answer...

"What's wrong Adam?" Said Eric

page 53

Adam: "Well Mr. K, nothing is wrong, my mind has been confused lately with several things."

Eric Smiled, loosen the brake of his wheel chair and came little closer to Adam, so their conversation take a more personal aspect...

"Tell me more about what's on your mind... what are the things that confuse you..." said Eric

Adam: "I'm 25 years old, I do consider myself a Good person, I don't cheat, I don't steal, and I don't take advantage of people... I work VERY HARD to earn my life... and yet I don't enjoy anything Even Close to the finer things in life... *sight*"

"And I look at Jerks who get to go out with the best looking girls and those girls worship them although they get treated way below what I have to offer... and on the Career level, Also Jerks and Bad people get to Boss around while I work my ass out... and finally Mrs. K says to me that I'm not advancing in my Career & Life because I'm 'NICE'... what the hell am supposed to do!!!" Adam then almost sniffed a tear from his eyes.

"Well Well Adam... I can feel where you're coming from" Said Eric while handing him a Tissue.

Eric "Let me tell you couple of things that would clarify what's happening with you... and with most of the 'NICE' people all around... "

"The modern Work - Love Game is Highly Complex, that's why it's normal you find difficulties understanding what should be considered as Common Sense...

If you watch Movies, you'll be fascinated by some Hollywood characters like James Bond... He's THE BAD BOY... You visualize the BOND married with 2 kids? Doing his own laundry or ironing his Tuxedo But yet he's very appealing and attractive to almost any girl.

So in General Bad boys whom girls like to be with... are simply Hollywood Bad Boys... Real Life Bad Boys are actually JERKS...

Now let me share with you what I have learned from years of experience in psychology of the human behavior... and what I'm going to tell you is a fact you and lots of others understood it Backward...

There are 3 layers of MEN... The Nice Guys, The Jerks and The Bad Boys. Unfortunately for the non-trained eye, they exist in that Order and from the Bottom up.

You have the Nice Guy in the Bottom, weightier they are at work talking to their boss or at a date... they are almost always considered as "BORING" and "Predictable"... they talk about Logical things and try to 99% of the time, they try to impress by bragging about themselves...

Bosses and Girls, can Smell when you're TRYING to impress them and trying to win their approval, as they will perceive you as Needy or insecure about yourself and that's a TURN OFF, so the more you push, the more they move away.

There's an Old saying about Banks: "They only want to lend you money when you're loaded already. If you genuinely need the money you can forget it."

Upper from the Nice Guys, you have the JERKS (and in your dictionary, if combined with good looks they are the BAD Boys you see going out with Great Looking Girls)... Jerks appeal to women more than nice guys, because mostly they aren't Boring; and more likely because they create an emotional roller coaster; they make their girls laugh, cry, put pressure on her and create a challenge for her to keep up.

Jerks normally don't care about what people think of them, they do whatever they like, whenever, and they will answer to no one; So they appear Confident and Self-assured and definitely INTERESTING.

Now if we combine these facets. Power, strength of character, confidence and an immensely interesting personality. That equals SEXY. Is it any wonder therefore that such types of guys often get the girls? It doesn't mean to say that we like them and it doesn't mean to say that this is fair or a good thing. But it can be nature's way."

Adam is almost breathless hearing what Eric is talking about, and somehow can relate strongly to the subject; he now understood what Samantha was talking about when she said that he is the "Nice Guy"... and also remembered his friend Casa with her "JERK" boyfriend and how all of that makes sense now... but then again, Eric was talking about 3 types of males... and he only heard 2 so far..

"What about the 3rd layer...?" asked Adam

Eric smiled from the ambition the Young Adam showed in wanting to hear the rest of the subject and then continued:

"In society, The Bad boys are the Leaders, they are the Alpha Males and people look up to them; They Poses a Balance of what the best of what the Nice guys have and what the Jerks accidently master.

The alpha male is confident, socially powerful, outgoing, fun, a leader, secure in himself, has high self-esteem, and is a guy who has his stuff together. He's able to joke around with women and be playful and in his Job he is an expert and is capable to drive his company forward.

He's the James Bond in Real Life... "

Adam felt deeply interested in the subject the more he heard Eric talking; and couldn't help not interrupting to ask:

"How can I become a Bad Boy...? I mean a James Bond in real life Mr. K?"

Eric laughed again, as he never heard this sentence before, he replied in a very calm way:

"Over decades of psychology, nearly 10s of 1000s of valuable books, theories and researches of famous psychologists... I can resume all of them to you in one sentence and one sentence only: *We become what we think about...*"

It's a very simple sentence yet not easy to implement as many people think differently from the inside out.

If you want to become the James Bond in Real Life, you have to first start thinking yourself as James Bond; and start analyzing what you like about him and find a way to create those qualities within you...

But that doesn't mean that you need to become a SPY to attract girls; start with the qualities that you can control; per example although Girls are attracted to Good Looks, Wealth, Social Status and Personality... some of them are not in your immediate control like wealth and good looks; so focus on changing your personality and how you react with girls first... and Put a goal to become wealthy and have a high Social Status... and you'll reach there."

Adam was Very happy to have had this conversation with Dr. K; he felt that he now have the knowledge and information that would change the course of his immediate and long term Future; so he Thanked Eric and just before he move toward the door Mrs. Kays entered the room;

Samantha: "What have we got here? You look like your smile can reach your ears... what happened?"

Adam: "I want to become James Bond Mrs. K, no more Mr. Nice Guy!"

Samantha wasn't expecting to hear such a phrase and looked at Eric who was almost falling on the ground from laughter.

"Dr. NO, what did you do to the Boy?" Said Samantha

"I simply taught him some rules from Russia with Love..." Said Eric while still laughing.

Adam was not very familiar with the James Bond Movies "Dr. No" & "From Russia with Love" but did understand what they were laughing at.

Samantha: "You are invited to Lunch with us 3 weeks from now, and I won't take NO for an answer."

Adam: "Certainly Mrs. K; Thank you So much for the invitation, and thank you Dr. K for the lovely time."

The young man left the K's glowing as if it was the Best night of his life... He rushed to his house, pulled out his Notebook and started writing...

Impress or go home

Practice, Practice, Practice

Those past weeks were tough on Adam, so many things he learned and lots of events happening around him that he can't ignore anymore, as if he was suddenly hitting Puberty all over again... Something's happening to him that he couldn't understand but definitely they can't pass by un-noticed...

He went out with one of his best friends one evening to grab a coffee and spend some quality time;

Adam: "What's wrong with me... my career looks like is going nowhere... I discovered lately that I'm a 'NICE' guy at work... and I can't find Love because I'm no James Bond and Mrs. K said that I don't have Balls"

MIKE: "That's the weirdest and sickest sentence I've ever heard... did you smoke something today?"

Adam Laughed and replied while smiling: "No no, it's just that I have been taking some work / life lessons from the Kays and in the process I'm looking differently at my life"

He started chatting with MIKE about the different things that have been happening to him, and about the Notebook that Mr. & Mrs. Kays have given to him.... They kept on talking for a while and MIKE was very entertained with Adam's Stories.

"Ok so let's divide your problems, you have bla bla bla... and then bla bla... and finally you need to add a 7 to your double Zeros." Smiled MIKE ironically

Adam: "Precisely!"

MIKE: "well you know what they say about 'Seven'... seven means Victory and Victory means Success... and you can't become successful with girls if you don't dare yourself to impress the Most beautiful girl in town"

Adam: "Huh?"

MIKE: "let me explain; The first rule is critical... if you want EVE Land to get impressed... you can try to impress them one by one... or Pick their Role Model and IMPRESS HER..."

Adam: "Ok?"

"So then, anything becomes possible for you..." said MIKE while winking at Adam and pointing to a Tall and great looking blonde sitting alone at the Coffee shop... and continues "Go Talk to her"

After like 10 tries, Adam managed to grab the courage to stand up and walked to where the young lady was sitting...

Adam: "Hi"

Erica: "Yes?"

Adam: "I was wondering if I can borrow your pen"

Erica: "Sure, but make it quick because I'm in the middle of something"

Adam went back to MIKE who was sitting trying to bare himself from laughing because Adam was ALL RED from shyness with a Pink Pen in his hand and looking at him with the "Now What Mr. Wise Guy?"

Adam went back to the girl and gave her back her Pink Pen.

Erica: "You know if you want to strike a conversation, there was tons of things you could've asked about like the book I was reading, the t-shirt that says 'what's your name' written all over it... etc. but you were more focusing on how I look rather than whom I might be..."

Adam was surprised from what the girl said to him, and he started apologizing for his behavior;

Erica: "Stop saying Sorry... you didn't do anything wrong, you were polite that's why I played along with you, but maybe you should've work on your voice loudness, as everyone in the coffee shop could've hear your conversation with your 'Expert' friend... "

Adam was now officially hitting a New LOW with the girls.

"Here's my advice to you Mr. but don't get the wrong idea… if you wanted to score like an NBA Player, you should practice to the extent that you can score a 3 points without getting distracted with the 0:03 Timing Left!" closed Erica and continued whatever she was doing.

Adam Grabbed MIKE and immediately left the coffee house;

MIKE: "Man, you were hilarious!"

Adam looked back at MIKE while trying to find a Big ROCK to hit him with it but breathed quietly and said: "It's easy for you to make jokes when you're sitting in the back seat and doing nothing… besides, I've never talked to a beautiful girl in my entire life, I shook like a Tree being hit by a BULL"

And out of a sudden… Adam just Stopped and looked up… he looked back at MIKE and said… "Wait! I think I have an idea!"

Adam: "I got nervous from trying to talk to a beautiful girl because I don't normally talk to attractive girls in my daily life. But what if I got to talk to very attractive girls, I would overcome that fear and will be about to Impress the Queen of EVE Land."

MIKE: "you're not making any sense for me… but I just heard too many words like 'beautiful girl' 'attractive girls' and 'impress the queen of Eve land' so I'M IN!"

Adam: "We're going to a Strip Club!"

MIKE: "What the Hell??"

Adam: "I'm always shy and nervous when there's a beautiful girl around and I almost never talk to any... so I need to get me some Practice!"

MIKE: "Bro, you're weird... but for the sake of our friendship... HELL YEAH... LET's GO Practice!!!!"

The 2 young men went to a strip club that had the most beautiful girls in the city; and sat at the bar;

Interestingly enough, most of the strippers were hanging around the customers talking and flirting with them while waiting for their dance turn in the purpose of creating "Demand Generation" so when it's the turn of one, lots of customers will start throwing money at her. Simply A different way of marketing for Tummies.

Now those girls started approaching Adam and MIKE, and started flirting and smooth talking...

"Well hello there! What's a handsome guy like you doing here... care for a lap dance?"

Adam had the actual striping activities on the least of his concerns... he wanted to practice being Close to a beautiful girl without getting confused and shy...

"What's... wha... whatt's a lap dddance?" nervously replied Adam

Then the girl grabbed his ear and talked to him for like 15 seconds... and left

Adam turned to MIKE who was already in a different world

"Did you see how much she was close to me? My heart almost stopped!!"

MIKE and Adam spent like 2 hours in that Club and spoken with almost every Stripper there... and by the time they were out... Adam was more comfortable talking to a beautiful girl than he ever imagined.

Adam decided to practice communicating with beautiful girls on daily basis, but in the real world and not in a strip club...

Days went by, Adam was becoming more and more a better communicator by simply deciding to practice communication with all sort of girls in the supermarket every night.

Adam didn't realize though that by practicing communicating with girls every night, his communication and presentation skills were getting better and better that he started improving in his Job at ABC Consulting and even keeping up with some of the best consultants while sipping a coffee at the common canteen.

One day Adam was waiting to use the elevator and one middle aged employee who looked like a client entered stood with him.

The gentleman was very classic in his appearance and was holding a book called "the 7 habits of highly effective people"; by a force of habit of trying to find anything to trigger a conversation with anyone, Adam happened to see the same book in the bookshelf in the supermarket he work in so he decided to stroke a question:

"Interesting book... I hear that it's one of the best sellers these days"

Gentleman: "indeed it is, I'm trying to apply all of the habits in my daily life"

Adam: "did you know that there's a sequel book to that called the 8th Habit?"

Gentleman: "aha... and what's the 8th Habit young man?"

Adam didn't have a clue what to tell the gentleman, because he didn't read either books and he only saw the book covers, but decided to bluff...

Adam smiled and replied back: "it's similar to the 5th habit in yours... what was it again?"

The gentleman smiled back and fell in the trap since he didn't yet finish the book...

"I'm Jonathan"

"I'm Adam"

"Pleasure to meet you Adam"

"Pleasure is mine Jonathan"

They both entered the elevator, and surprisingly Jonathan pressed the 34rd Floor. So Adam clicked on the first floor out, since Jonathan can either be one of the Executives of ABC Consulting or an important client and bluffing with him in this case was inappropriate not to mention that it can dangerously ruin his career. He played it cool until he was out of the elevator.

2 hours later, Adam's Desk phone rang.

Adam: "ABC Consulting... This is Adam"

Caller: "Hi Adam, I'm Philippe from Management"

Adam: "Oh Hi Mr. Philippe, what can I do for you?"

Philippe: "have you had a conversation with someone named Jonathan today in the Elevator?"

Adam started seeing his dreams breaking apart and his hopes of any type of promotion vanishing before his eyes... but he kept his feelings to himself and answered back:

"Yes sir, we had a conversation in the elevator about books"

Philippe: "I don't know what type of books you talked about, but I want you to get your Ass into my office in the next 5 minutes..."

Adam confirmed his Fears... he is definitely fired... so he went up to Philippe's office.

Philippe was the President & COO of ABC Consulting and one of the most influential people in the company.

Philippe: "do you know who Jonathan is?"

Adam: "No Sir"

Philippe: "John is one of the biggest potential clients we may ever have; we've been trying to get business from him for a long time now... he has always been TOUGH negotiator and a sharp in his demands"

Philippe: "So John was meeting with the board today in order for us to put an effort to collectively win him over… and while normally we suffer to make him convinced in our approaches; this time was different… he said YES with one condition"

Adam: "Which condition Sir?"

Philippe: "that he picks his own consultant, and guess whom he picked?"

Adam: "amm… I don't know"

Philippe: "He showed us his teeth for the first time in a first time laugh, and asked for you to be the primary consultant on the project"

Adam: "ME? But I'm not even a Consultant!!"

Philippe: "You WERE THE CONDITION for us to win a 28 Million $ Deal... John said to us that it requires BALLS to be able to look him in the eye and tell him 'I don't buy what you're selling' which was a straight hit to his ego that no one got the nerves to do it and that you Did without Blinking an Eye."

Adam: "ME?? Without blinking an EYE!!!!"

Philippe: "Yes You... I don't know how you did it... But Son, I apologies that I joked when I said that you're the Late Hidden Talent to Samantha the other day... Your Skills have made us win a major customer, you achieved in minutes what we tried to achieve in the past 2 years... Hat's Off Mr. Adam!"

Adam kept starring in Shock at Philippe congratulating him on a Job Well done... while he didn't do anything but PRACTICING Communication with the purpose of enhancing his chances in impressing a girl.

He went back home early that day, didn't want to go anywhere else and decided to take some time to think for himself and reflect on what is happening with him...

For the past couple of years he has been so much busy with the regular office work that he almost forgot that his main purpose of getting that Entry-level job at ABC Consulting is a mean to a purpose of one day becoming one of their Consultants... And now that he's hit by an opportunity to prove himself and change the course of his life & career, he had no idea what to do next nor any idea on what Consulting was!

Adam Kept Thinking till it HURT...

He then opened his notebook and started writing...

Adam fell asleep while he didn't finish his note.

Start Well but End Better

The Test

Adam woke up feeling little tiered; He has been sleeping since 8:00 PM.

He went to the office to find everyone almost "Waiting" for him to show up; apparently News travel fast these days, especially when they fall down from a higher floor.

Everyone was looking at Adam as if he was an Alien that did NOT come in Peace... Everyone except Jessica.

Jessica gazed at him in a Pride look. He smiled at her and just when he was about to go and talked to her....

"I Heard about your Heroic Act Mr. Adam" Joe said to Adam while intercepting the connection between Him and Jessica.

Adam: "Hi Joe"

Joe: "I told you that I will keep an eye on you... but now I assure you that I will keep BOTH eyes on you."

Adam got nervous and in an upset tone replied back to Joe

"What's your problem Joe? Didn't your Mommy ever taught you not to talk to people when your mouth is full"

Joe, who normally is a bad mood, got upset at his turn and Frowned at Adam

"My Mouth is full? Full of What?"

"Your Mouth is Full of Shhhhiii......" and just before Adam Continue the sentence he realized that he's making a mistake that he will regret it later on… so he decided to end this argument while he can and get out of Joe's way.

Adam, who didn't have the chance to even sit on his desk, found himself walking out the office and down to the nearest coffee shop;

As he was walking into the coffeehouse, he felt like he saw a familiar face, it was that girl from last time sitting there with her book and Pink pen.

Adam who just had a fight with his Boss, looked at the Cute Blonde girl and in 3 seconds he found himself walking towards her.

Adam: "Hey, what's your Name?"

Erica: "I Beg your Pardon! Who do you think you are to come talk to me like that?"

Adam: "The Book by your bag has a catchy title, but we both know that you haven't read a single chapter in it. It's still very well catered since the last time I saw you 3 weeks ago... your eyeglasses have no medical lenses in them which imply you're wearing them to draw the attention that you're a smart girl. And finally pretending that you're an Espresso person while it seems to me that your cup is Cold and Untouched... So judging from all that and considering the time of the day... I am cutting through the chase, what's your Name?"

Erica felt insulted and was about to throw the untouched espresso to his face, but yet couldn't stop admiring the BALLS this stranger showed by talking to her this way.

Erica: "This Book is Called Social Intelligence and the book I was reading 3 weeks ago, was called Emotional Intelligence, and they are both for the Same Author and have almost the same cover design for the un-trained eye.

The glasses I wear have what they call "Progressive Lenses" that are wear by patients who have presbyopia —a vision condition marked by a decrease in the ability to focus sharply on nearby objects. There are no visible lines separations so the eyes would be seen very clearly behind them.

And "Finally", a young man tried to hit on me by buying me a cup of espresso thinking that I would invite him to join me, so I left it un-touched....

See you again in 3 weeks stranger... "

Adam could almost burry himself alive from Shame, he didn't know what to do and for the second time in less than 3 hours, he found himself leaving a place without even sitting down.

As he was crossing the street, when his phone ringed, it was ABC Consulting number on the Caller ID, so Adam was hesitating to answer knowing that the 3rd time is charm in this messed up day.

Voice on the end of the Call: "Where the hell are you?"

Adam: "That's not of your freaking concern!"

"You have a lot of nerves to answer me back like that; I'll get to that later, I need your Ass in my Office in 20 minutes! Our meeting with Jonathan is in less than an hour and you need to be briefed."

Adam noticed that the voice on the other End was more PHILIPPE than Joe and replied back "I'm sorry sir I thought you were someone else, I'll be in your office in 10 minutes Top."

9 ½ minutes later, Adam was in Philippe's office, he was welcomed by

a nasty look from Philippe himself and the other part of the team.

Philippe: "Have you study the case well?"

Adam: "What case?"

Philippe: "I sent you an email yesterday, informing you that we will start the initial meeting with Jonathan and his team today at 10 AM and a full document on the project"

Adam was Frozen in his place: "Yesterday!!"

Philippe: "Yes Yesterday, and I also sent you a reminder this morning... didn't you check your email?"

"Off course, I was just messing around with you... have you printed a copy so

I review it before our meeting?" Adam Bluffed one more time to save his ass.

He started reading and reading and reading... until he almost memorized the whole 20 pages document.

At 10 am Sharp, Jonathan and his Business Planning Manager entered the Conference room.

And just when this day couldn't get any worse... it turned out that the Business Planning Manager of Mr. Jonathan was actually the girl from the Coffee shop; who was definitely taking her time and sipping her coffee until her meeting starts across the street.

Philippe welcomed his guests and invited them to sit down; John walked towards Adam and warmly shook his hand

"I'm keeping an eye on you..." smiled John

"You don't want to know what happened to the last person who said that to me... " Replied Adam with sarcasm.

John Sat down and introduced Erica to Adam

"This young man is a very intellectual and sharp Consultant, and I believe he will be a great help to our project; Adam this is Erica Smith my Business

Planning Manager and Executive Assistant"

Erica: "it's a Pleasure to meet you Mr.....??"

"Just call me Adam." Adam replied with the spirit of a man who has nothing to lose.

John: "So any new Books you've been reading lately Adam?"

Adam: "Well you know the past few weeks were busy, but I heard that the Book "emotional intelligence" was quite a book"

John: "Why it's a fascinating Book! Erica kept talking about it for a while and she used to take it with her wherever she goes!"

Adam found the perfect time to strike back...

"That's Great Erica, I see you have a good taste of books like your Boss; have you read the other Book by the same Author, I believe it's called "Social Intelligence"?" Adam said while holding his Devilish Smile...

Erica nervously: "I bought it yesterday... but unfortunately haven't got the time to read it yet... have you read it Adam?"

Adam intelligently switched to Jonathan, and asked:

"Mr. Jonathan, we have a long discussion ahead, can I interest you with some coffee?"

John: "That's very thoughtful of you Adam"

And quickly Adam took the phone and spoke with the receptionist while maintaining eye contact with Erica: "2 ESPRESSO for Mr. Jonathan and his Assistant Please!"

Erica was about to blow up from FURY but yet she was impressed by seeing Adam evolve from Being the Nice guy, to becoming a Jerk and then Graduating to become an Alpha Male!

The meeting started, and since it was the initial meeting only, there was really not much input required from ABC Consulting, but more of a get to know the ground and establish the business relationship; so it progressed smoothly over the next hour and a half.

And the end John thanked Philippe for his time, and shacked hands with Adam and told him: "You must visit our offices soon; I'm looking forward to discussing some ideas with you"

Adam: "it will be my pleasure Mr. Jonathan, now if you excuse me I have another meeting that I need to attend."

Adam intentionally left before he even talk to Erica again, who almost broke her glasses while packing her things trying to walk out.

It was quite a day for Adam... He finished his pending things from his desk and kept on doing some additional tasks trying to move his mind somewhere else... he kept working and working till he noticed that everyone else has already left and he is already late on his second job;

In the night shift that day Adam felt as if he was taking part of a Music Video where he was standing still and everything around him was moving fast...

He opened his notebook and started writing...

Climbing the Ladder

The Interview

The next morning, Adam received an email from STEVE, the HR director at ABC Consulting suggesting to have an interview the Following week for a Consultant position at the firm;

Adam was surprised as he didn't apply to any job openings in the firm, but after the week he passed through, nothing was un-expected, so he answered back confirming the meeting for the interview to Steve.

It was already 3 weeks, the Kays were expecting Adam for Lunch, so he passed by a flower shop and brought Mrs. K some daisies and rushed to tell her about the last experiences he had and about the news that he will be interviewed for the consultant position.

For the first time since he met the Kays, it was Adam who was doing the talking; he was super enthusiastic, he kept talking and talking about every single detail that happened with him that he barely touched his dish!

"Well Well, some week for you" said Mrs. K

Dr. K: "I wouldn't call it beginner's Luck, because that would imply that

Adam should've been doing the first step INTENTIONNALLY as a Beginner... so let's call it just Luck"

Adam: "Well, when I come to think about it, none of that made sense at the time, I just went with the flow and got where it took me. But now that I have an interview that I Actually know about beforehand; I'm freaking out!"

Samantha: "Well interviews never get easier, you will need to be well prepared for that if you want to ACE your way into the consulting business in that Top Firm"

Adam: "How do I prepare? I have been working at the firm for a while now, so I'm not a stranger... I will just need to dress up and show up to the interview, Right??"

Eric: "If what you just said works, everyone should get promoted easily and a genitor can become a VP, since he knows Every DIRTY detail of the company" and he started laughing.

Adam got the message, so he asked the Kays to help him out in the preparation.

Dr. K who is an experienced Psychologist started explaining the interview process from a different point of view:

"I'm sure Samantha will add loads of advices to what I'm going to tell you, but I would like to highlight this first,

Job Interviews are very similar to Relationship "Interviews" now It's obvious that a Job Interview is way different from dating... but here's the thing... they are both a way to define a successful engagement between a person and a relationship... whether it's a personal relationship or a business relationship.

So let's say there should be a perfect interview... I would ask my HR director to see a candidate twice a week for year.. Have lunch or coffee and then get to know him/her on many aspects and see her good / bad qualities throughout the year... and then decide if the candidate fits the position or not... wouldn't that be cool... unfortunately that doesn't happen... because neither can afford that... at the end each have barely 15 minutes to either impress or not the person standing before them ...

And after long research... Companies who have long history of Successful HR can spot a good candidate in the first 3 minutes of the interview and they have been 90+% accurate in that... "

Samantha commented: "What Eric means in the Job interview process similarity to dating is very simple actually... The interviewer is a Man or a Woman sitting at the other end of the table, just like when you want to go and meet a girl somewhere... the same rules applies; at the end you're getting interviewed and you're getting interviewed by a Person... not a Company"

Adam: "Ok that's interesting, so if that person doesn't like me, he will reject my application and the opposite is true?"

Samantha: "not necessarily, but the opposite is true... meaning that if the interviewer doesn't like you, your chances are related to lots of other factors (like other candidates, your qualifications vs. needs of the job... etc.), but if he do like you, some qualities will stand up by themselves and you're automatically different from other candidates."

Dr. Kays: "True! now the sad truth is that we fancy people who act/ look like other people we like, love or have loved. So don't take rejection personally! Half the time is their past or issue. (You're too good for them.

you look like the ex who ran away with the best friend...)

But putting the pre-judgment of backward similarities aside, Samantha is Right about the Differentiation part; Let me explain to you...

Consider the recruiter a gorgeous girl getting picked up at a bar, she does get approached by several guys just like the recruiter gets candidates to evaluate; after a while, the different candidates will all look the same, talk the same and act the same... so little difference in efforts will be made in judging them beyond the first 2-3 minutes (or even less!), the rest will be either Protocol or simply courtesy. "

Adam: "Interesting"

Dr. Kays Continued "So let's say you've heard all the terms, you've witnessed all the tricks, what options do you have Adam?"

Adam: "mmmmm, well if a person has heard them all before, I would first try to come up with Better versions?"

Samantha: "I like that... but if you're trying to TOP your ancestors, you've raised the bar higher now... so you will need to keep up with that..."

"Or I can try something completely different" continued Adam

Dr. K: "Different is better than raising the bar, because being different will mark you in the "Innovator category" rather than in the bragger.

But don't be the Accidental innovator... plan your approach very well, and that's what Samantha meant by being Ready

"

Adam: "Planning my Approach... wait a minute, how can I plan the unknown... I need to react to the interviewer, beyond that what's your name / where are you from? ... I can't prepare for anything!"

Mrs. K: "Well Young Adam, Let's Not forget something important here...

Your situation would've been difficult if you're getting interviewed in a Small or a Medium size Company... Companies like ABC Consulting have a Mature structure in HR, so mostly they will have rules, regulations and even pre-defined process in recruiting, so you will have 80%

chance to be asked very common questions and the 20% left will be very ABC Specific"

Adam: "Huh?"

Mrs. K: "HR is a discipline like any other major studied in universities, it's not rocket science and it's not a SECRET... yet lots of candidates Over-Estimate the questions and underestimate the value of the answers they give. So I will give you these 3 simple rules that will help you prepare.

Rule #1: Do an internet research or get a book on HR / interviews, I can recommend lots of good ones. Read about the Questions often asked in the interview and what the message the interviewer is seeking from you.

Rule #2: Do a big research on the Company & the position you're applying to

Rule #3: Make sure you're marketing yourself well... well done CV, mind your Business etiquette and VALUE Yourself
"

Samantha looked at Eric and asked him: "Honey, I remember you once told me something about the body language in interviews"

Dr. K: "I have told you, talking to an interviewer obey the same rules as trying to impress a girl, it has a lot to do with body language and how you 'Talk' to her "

Adam: "I'm sorry Dr. K, I'm not following here"

Dr. K: "Let me explain more about this,

We communicate and send messages with our Body more than our words can say, that's why you find yourself waving with your hand when you're talking on your cellphone especially when there was no one around.

Every one of us, has a magnificent power called the Sub-Conscious mind, now I won't go deep in here, but this subconscious mind is responsible mainly for the body language that you don't voluntarily do.

And guess who are the Most NATURALLY-BORN-Experts in Body Language?"

Adam: "The CIA?"

Dr. K laughed and reply: "The CIA definitely know the Science of the mind and the body language but there's some who naturally know these things... WOMEN!"

Adam: "Women?"

Mrs. K: "Eric has a point, us Women, we have a natural Radar for stuff like Lying, nervousness, love, guilt... etc."

Dr. K: "Here's a tip on this: Every human has a pre-programmed way to understand body language signals, some do this consciously (mostly women) and some just got a strange feeling that they cannot understand (where some call it a Hunch or a good/bad feeling)"

Adam: "so that was interesting but I really don't know how to apply what you both just said."

Dr. K: "First you need to make / keep eye contact at all time with the interviewer or even with the girl you want to meet"

Mrs. K: "if you don't know where to look, try to look at the center of the face right between the eyes"

Dr. K: "try to keep your hands in a position in front of you where your fingers can barely touch each other's."

Mrs. K: "Yes that is good… you can form a Diamond Shape with your hands. and remember don't Ever Cross your Hands while you're talking to anyone… it signify that you're being defensive and if you saw the interviewer doing that… try to ask him/her to hand you a pen or anything just so he un-cross his hands and he be 'open' to listening to you"

The conversation went on and on about different techniques and tips and tricks to success in the interview.

Adam thanked the Kays and went on to his path to discover how to ACE an interview.

All he did remember from that HR was a science, the interview is like Picking up a girl and he needs to mind his body language.

He Spent the next day's practicing his upcoming interview, reading books and researching the company and how to be a Consultant.

One day he was out with his friend Nour when they saw a nice attractive girl sitting at the bar with couple of her girlfriends' chit chatting.

Over their first 15 minutes at the Pub, that group of girls have already had 3-4 pickup attempt from random guys;

Nour: "you look distracted... what's wrong?"

Adam: "I've been reading a lot lately, and I want to start practicing for my next interview"

Nour: "Here!!"

Adam: "Oh Yes! Just watch and learn"

Nour: "That's gotta be good!"

After several eye contacts and hidden smiles, Adam walked toward the group of girls, he has had a lot of experience talking to girls before, but this time he wanted it to be different.

Right towards the middle, maintaining Eye contact and with the right James Bond Body language, he said the Most Unbreakable pick up line ever, with the right Voice tune...

Adam: "Hi"

Girl: "hi"

Adam: "I like you and I'd like to get to know you"

The girl looked at him with a flashing surprise, he didn't break his eye contact and he sounded definitely a nice hybrid between 100% Honest,

Confident and Mr. knows what he wanted...

Girl: "What makes you think that I would like to get to know you?"

Adam: "Because you already made up your mind about that before I even say Hi"

Girl: "oh really??"

Adam: "Besides, you deserve better than the last 10 guys who tried hitting on you in the past 30 minutes, what's your name?"

Girl: "I'm Kelly... and you are?"

"Different..." Smiled Adam Mysteriously

They say the first 3-4 seconds are crucial because one needs to decide to take a move immediately... the second stage he needs to keep up for 3 – 4 minutes and after that... it's nature's way.

Adam started several interesting conversations with the group and invited Nour to join and they spent some nice time;

Unfortunately Kelly and her friends were too much of the alcoholic type and less on the social one, so the evening didn't end quite as expected and Adam and Nour left without even keeping any of their phone numbers.

2 more days passed by and Adam found himself looking at the mirror, preparing himself for the interview.

He dressed as if he was already hired as a consultant, and printed out his resume and placed it in a nice transparent envelope, and at exactly 9:00 AM, Adam was in the Conference room waiting for the interview to start.

Adam was prepared to most of the scenarios available but one.... That the interviewer would be more than 1 person at the same time.

Steve, Miranda and Josh sat across from Adam who was a bit surprised and confused about how to begin but was saved by his skills earned in the last few months.

"They stopped making those types of Ties, so that must be from a limited edition" Said Adam to Josh,

Josh: "Indeed, it's a private collection that was on sale and I took the opportunity to own it... your Tie also looks distinguished, where did you get it from?"

Adam was not much of suits person, so the tie was borrowed from one of his friends, and while he has very little knowledge on the subject it happened that for some reason he saw Josh's Tie in an advertisement while he was researching, so he answered

"It's also from a Private collection, I saw it in my friend's closet and I said to myself I need to have it!"

Steve "Interesting... You look like a determinant person Mr. Adam"

Adam has read every book he could've found on the HR Topic and the FIRST thing he learned was that Questions and Thoughts don't come from Nowhere, so every question needs to have a message expected behind it.

Adam: "Determination to becoming better is a virtue, so yes I'm guilty as charged"

Miranda: "What makes you think you're good enough to be a consultant in our firm?"

Adam: "I'm confident about my qualifications and my determination to become the best consultant this firm has ever known."

Steve: "you don't have a consulting experience, so again why should we consider your application?"

Adam: "my actual application to the opening, was simply to reply to your email with my interest, and that places me ahead of other candidates who had to 'Learn about the opening', 'Apply' and 'get selected' for an interview"

Steve, Miranda and Josh were impressed by the confidence Adam showed in his interview and kept on asking hard questions trying to push him to a corner but he was anticipating every move and every try.

1 hour and a half later, they were all done with the interview, Adam thanked everyone for their time and effort and left the floor to go back to his day-to-day job in the data entry department.

Adam ended his day holding the Notebook in his Second Job, reading some pages, and then started to write...

Who's Different?

Meet your Boss

Adam Got Accepted to Work as a Consultant in ABC Consulting, and His life took a drastic change afterwards; He no longer had to work 2 shifts so he resigned from his second job at the supermarket;

The Kays were very proud of him and kept on coaching and guiding him throughout his new path.

5 Years Later...

Adam gave more attention to his health, and started working out more frequently, changed the way he dress and he became even more attractive than ever, spent much time educating himself & periodically feeding his brain by reading books, taking extra-courses and attending seminars.

Adam has become a Senior Consultant at ABC Consulting, learned so much on the Job, he simply Loved what he was doing...

On a Personal Level, Adam apparently took the Myth of *THE ONE* more seriously than he should, that he couldn't hold on to ONE serious relationship over that time; his continuously improved skills increased his dates and placed him in a new category of Men, he dated different types of girls, from the Hot and Irresistible ones to the Highly-educated ones, to Simple and Normal ones.

On his friends' side, his close friends (MIKE, Nour & BACH) remained by his side;

MIKE shifted from being a practitioner lawyer to become the General Manager of an Advertising Company; Nour continued being a Mechanical engineer but followed his passion in Copywriting so he took jobs on the side; BACH has relocated to a Different region and took a Job in the Marketing & Banking while he never let go of his Sports passion and continued playing in some local games whenever he traveled back to visit his home country.

During his travels and the years passing by, Adam made new Friends and lots of connections in different countries, to name a few: Eddy, Wess, Nadine and Jasmine.

Adam never missed one opportunity to stay in touch with the Kays; although his time became slightly tighter than before, but he continued getting trained and coached on different life, love and Work topics; and certainly never left a chance to keep recording all his learning in his precious Notebook.

One day he was coming back from a long trip in the West, and passed by the Office; he bumped into his newly appointed manager, a strong and confident Woman-Manager, Lila.

Lila: "Hi Adam, How was your trip? You look very tiered"

Adam: "it was a long one, I'm used to long trips but this one was just quite exhausting... but we achieved good results."

Lila: "I like the Sound of the phrase... tell me more about the good results!"

Adam: "I saved our customer at least 35% of losses and managed to make the curve of his sales corrected to bring positive results in the immediate future"

Lila: "I wouldn't call that 'good results'... But you're on the right track... we'll talk more afterwards"

Adam did like Lila, but for some reason, she had a thing with the word "*appreciation*", it seems that nothing is ever good enough for her....

Adam was dating at the time an Airline Hostess, Natasha, whom he met while spending time at the airport more than he spent time home.

Adam and Natasha were too much of a casual dating with casual add-on emotions, but they didn't share love, at least not from Adam's Side; he enjoys spending time with Natasha, but she was more of a *Drama Queen* than a *Whatever-is-the-Antonym-of-Drama-is Princess*, although she knew that Adam was faithful to her or at least to what they have, she kept on making his life challenging rather than in the peace of mind phase.

8:00 pm, Sunday night, Adam and Natasha had dinner's reservation at Mr. Steak downtown.

Natasha: "I simply hate what I'm doing, every day I do almost the same thing, I even Hate performing the 'To Fasten your Seatbelt and to un-Fasten your Seatbelt' Every single day... I don't know how I can survive that..."

Adam: "You're smart, why do you keep doing that if you don't like it, why don't you quit and look for something else?"

Natasha: "I do love traveling and seeing new countries and meeting new people, I just hate to fake smiling and to act like I'm always happy..."

Adam: "you don't have to fake smiling; if you're not happy simply don't smile"

Natasha: "someone tried to hit on me the other day, I told my supervisor and instead of him doing something about it, he just laughed and told me to take it easy... can you imagine he told me to take it easy!"

Adam: "it's ok, you're a cute girl so it's normal for that to happen, and what do you expect your supervisor to do, the flight would end eventually and you won't see that Punk ever again… Why make a fire?"

Natasha nervously: "See, you *always* do that, you *never* listen to what I say!"

Adam: "Whaaa..? I *Never* Listen? *Always*? I heard every sentence you said and I even offered to help out"

Natasha: "no you were not, you were staring at that skinny Blonde all the time!"

Adam: "Blonde? What Blonde?"

Adam turned his head to notice a gorgeous blonde sitting right across from them with shiny lipsticks and gazing at him.

"I didn't even see her!!" said Adam

Natasha: "Come on she couldn't stop looking at you all night"

Adam: "how is that my fault, I didn't even notice her"

Natasha: "You're never around when I need you, and you never do the things that I want you to do..."

Adam: "You Work as an Airline Hostess and I'm NEVER around for you? And what's with these things you keep bringing up every time we go out about me not doing the things I'm 'Supposed' to do with you? "

Natasha: "if a man likes a woman he should simply KNOW how to act with her... he shouldn't wait for her to TELL him what to do or what to say!"

Adam: "Listen Natasha, we have a Beautiful thing going on between us, why do you insist on pushing the Drama into it every time... I do have lots of issues on my mind from Work and stuff... why can't we have a

NORMAL relationship like any couple would have?"

Natasha: "Bccause you're not honest with me, you keep telling me that you have issues at work and I YET never hear you talk about them... and every time I tell you to do something that would benefit you and our relationship you simply get upset as if I'm asking you to run Naked in the park. I can't take it anymore with you... I think we need some space."

Adam: "How on earth did this evening ended up this way... we were supposed to be having a nice Steak Dinner... you know something have it your way... I can't live with your Drama either... CHECK PLEASE!"

Adam and Natasha left each in his own way that evening; she couldn't stand him not doing enough efforts for their relationships and he couldn't stand her Drama-Princess Star Role that she keeps playing every once and a while.

The second day, Adam went to work, feeling down from what happened last night... he Saw Lila, waiting for him.

Lila: "Good Morning Adam, how are we today?"

Adam: "I've had better days..."

Lila: "I have a big assignment for you this week; you need to build the new sales strategy of FDT Corporation's new Mobile Devices in the Chinese Market;"

Adam: "That's easy, I don't need a week, I can tell you from now... They will spend half a Million on Marketing and Advertising, 3 Million on Production, another half and Million on Distribution, 250K for our consultancy, and in the end they will sell less than 2 Million so my advice to them would be to throw 2 Million Dollars in the sea and market their devices somewhere else and they would still make more money."

Lila: "That's not going to happen… I want you to find a SOLUTION, I don't want us to lose this client because you're guessing your way around…"

Adam: "I'm not guessing, it's Logical that the market of mobile devices in China is too mature to allow the introduction of another Mobile Devices player who has been barely PLAYING in his own Back Yard."

Lila: "Remember that this 250k consultancy is paying your paycheck, and if we're not going to get it because you're too tired to work this week, I'll personally make sure that you will be looking for a cashier position in Burger King to pay your bills."

Adam spent the rest of the day very tensed... He was determined that he wants what's best for his customers for the sake of keeping the company's reputation of being the trusted advisors for 1000s of corporations worldwide. But yet, he couldn't say no to his boss, or else he would lose his job or at least get a HELL of a Time in his Job till the Cashier position at "The House of the Whooper" becomes more appealing...

That week was barely moving, Adam spent sleepless nights trying to figure out a way for FDT Corp. to have a serious market penetration and make some profit on the way.

At the end, he handed a file full of paper with numbers almost singing to Lila.

Lila: "Now that's better... Buy yourself a Vegetable Noodles Plate on me for lunch..." and she turned to her office laughing.

Adam have had such a terrible week both personally and professionally so he needed some advice from the couple who never let him down. The Kays!

"Oh My! It seems you've had quite a week young Adam" Said Mrs. Kays while offering Adam some Tea and Homemade Cookies.

Adam: "What is it with Women? At work or at home, a Man either do it their way... or they manage to make His Life Hell on Earth"

Dr. Kays Laughed and grabbed Samantha to his arms and kissed her hand: "Well Adam, you know what they say, you can't live with them and you can't live without them"

Adam: "There you said it... you CAN'T LIVE..."

Eric: "Let me explain this to you, we are first talking about 2 cases here, they may look similar but they different in reality... although we're talking about the battle of the Sexes, but that's only in one case, your case with your girlfriend... the other battle has nothing to do with the Sexes but it's more of a Boss/Employee thing."

Samantha: "Eric is right; having a Female Boss is certainly different that having a Male boss, but the Boss/Employee relationship is always awkward to begin with."

Dr. Kays: "I didn't want to interrupt your story with Natasha with my comments because I actually enjoyed listening to it, you just have to have my experience to be able to see how Normal that was, and how 1000s of couples worldwide have the SAME thing happening with them every day."

Adam: "Huh?"

Dr. Kays: "Oh yes my dear Adam; Men and women are Different... neither is better or worse... just different.

And even better than that... Men and Women are SUPPOSED TO be Different, and these are fundamental differences not Optional differences meaning that you can't choose WHEN you want to accept that difference and when not, yet very few admit that and as a result we often find relationships are Filled with friction and un-necessary stress.

"

Samantha: "Exactly, and believe me, lots of relationships FAIL just because men expect Women to act like Men and Women expect Men to React like Women."

Adam: "bla bla bla... Different... Men are Men, Women are Women... I still don't get you"

Dr. Kays: "I know it's a little bit hard to understand... but I promise you, once you start understanding the main differences between Men and Women, Boss and Employee, your life will become Easier"

Samantha: "True"

Dr. Kays: "The Male and Female Brains are different, their hormones are different, along with so many other things... and what I will tell you Adam right now can and will apply to most Men out there and same thing goes on Natasha and 99% of other women in the world.

Well at a glance; Women talk for different reasons than men... If a woman is bothered by something, she will try to relief her stress by Talking about the subject out... her brain simply store the information differently than Men... she needs to

CONFIRM the matter in her Brain (like the Save Button on your computer software) by just talking about it... while a man saves information in his brain Silently and he can be treating his problems in complete silence.

So what happened at dinner with you and Natasha, she was talking to you about her problems... to relief her stress and in return what did you do?"

Adam: "I was reacting to her sentences... show her that I care and that I have full attention."

Dr. K: "Nope... that wasn't what you were doing... you were offering her SOLUTIONS... because that's what Men do"

Adam: "What was I supposed to do then??"

Samantha: "Simply stay quiet, listen and CONFORT her... No Solutions"

Adam: "but if she was not asking for my advice, why is she telling me these things?"

Dr. K: "Women sometimes just need to talk about their problems, while men's conversations always have an Intro, a Clear Point and a Conclusion... Men don't talk just for the sake of talking"

Adam: "but she kept jumping from one subject to the other and started accusing me that I was looking at the blonde girl across the room while I swear I didn't even notice her..."

Dr. K: "I Believe you, that's something Women has and unfortunately they don't know they have it... an enhanced Peripheral vision"

Samantha: "That's exciting, I didn't know about that... Tell me more"

Dr. K: "Well Women can see 45 degrees height and almost 180 degrees wide... meaning that a woman can spot notice the color of your boots without even blinking her eyes... and he can notice someone passing by without even turning her Head..."

Samantha: "Hahahah... True!"

Dr. K: "While Men on the other hand have a Tunnel vision, meaning that they only view forward, that's why you didn't notice the blonde without turning your head..."

Adam: "umm... ok... what about when she started telling me that she can't stand that I don't just KNOW how to deal with her..."

Dr. K: "That's also a major issue between men and women, a Woman think that a Man should Genetically know how to deal with her, know her needs, how she likes to be treated, watching the smallest details of her life... While Men are not equipped to see/hear details and they need to be trained in a way on how to read the signs on how things should work out with Women"

Adam: "I'm not following... "

Dr. K: "Men By Nature, Hates Criticism, while a woman always try to 'Guide' her man, he feels that she's telling him 'you're not good enough'... so if she knew How to draw his attention to the things that she likes... and he put more efforts on understanding how she thinks... their lives would've been much easier"

Adam: "but Her Words were very specific Dr. K... I did hear every word she was saying"

Eric: "Well here's another Sad truth that men don't understand about women... a Woman most of the times say things that she doesn't mean; she focuses more on the feeling associated with the sentence rather on the sentence itself; while a man interpreted her WORDINGS one by one... And answer to each sentence... which is what happened with both of you when you were arguing"

Adam stood in Silence for a moment... then said: "but how do you explain what she said at the end about her needing a Space from our relationship..."

Dr. K Smiled and said: "I'll tell you the Technical Term and Mrs. K can give you an example"

Samantha: "I don't get it, an example of what exactly?"

Eric: "Tell him about the time when you bought this beautiful red dress that you never wear... while you always 'Take' my opinion about which one to choose"

Then Samantha smiled and started telling Adam the story...

"We were still newlywed, Every time we had an occasion I used to come to Eric and ask him which Dress I should wear, the Red one or the X one.

Eric always suggests the Red one, and I keep insisting that the other dress would look better and we end up fighting because Eric shouts 'why do you even bother asking me about it if you're not going to even consider my opinion...' and only years later that I actually worn that dress... "

Dr. K: "And that's my Dear Adam is called the IN-DIRECT Speech that Women always use"

Adam: "Indirect Speech?"

Dr. K: "Oh Yeah... most of the time, a Woman will ask you a question, suggest a sentence, while she already know the answer she is expecting from you... and the funny thing is that you need to KNOW what she is waiting for and give it to her otherwise you're in trouble"

Adam: "and how is that related to my Dinner with Natasha?"

Dr. K: "She was expecting from you to tell her that you're in Love with her and that you care about her beyond what just happened and that you won't stand still and allow the 'Space' to happen."

Adam: "Really? And I what... Blew it?"

Dr. K: "Women have a Special Language men need to speak, and special actions to be done for them."

Adam: "can you summarize that in like 1 sentence?"

Dr. K: "of course... it all goes down to this sentence:

Men feel motivated when they feel NEEDED and Women when they feel CHERISHED."

Adam: "Wow that's deep... and it makes sense"

Dr. K: "I'm going to bring you couple of books so you read on the subject."

Adam: "Thank you Dr. K"

Mrs. Kays: "Well your other issue, is not very different in Core... because when you understand the main differences between a Boss and an Employee and how both think... lots of Things would start to make sense... and the VERY Same sentence Eric just Told you I would quote talking about the Boss / Employee...

A Boss is Motivated, when he/she feels NEEDED and an employee when he/she feels CHERISHED."

Adam: "So the Boss is the MAN here?"

Samantha: "not necessarily... it's just that both are Different and they are Supposed to be different... the Boss most of the time expect his employees to view their actions like he does, and to take the initiative and responsibility as if they Own the company... while that's not genetic for employees, but does require lots of guidance and training simply like how a Woman expect her man to Simply KNOW how to act and react."

Adam: "I see... but I'm the one doing all the trouble and my manager do the complaining and that the NOT Enough things on me... how can that be fair?"

Samantha: "let me tell you how a typical day would look like back when I was CEO"

Adam: "Ah yes, you were CEO!"

Samantha: "Yes, I was CEO in a 3,000 Employees Sized Corporation before I retire."

Adam: "Nice... Tell me about your Typical Day"

Samantha: "

A typical Day would look like:

Meet the Marketing Director to discuss the programme for launching a new product

The HR Director to decide how best to reorganize the distribution department

The production director to ask him why costs per unit of output are going up and what he is going to do about that

The finance director to review the latest set of management account before the next board meeting.

May have had to meet with a Journalist to be interviewer about how the company is going to deliver better results next year

Lunch can be taken to meet with a major customer and the evening spent at a Business dinner.

The above can always be categorized into:

Getting things done (Planning ahead, maintaining momentum and making things happen)

Finding out what is going on

Reacting to new Situations and problems

Responding to demands and requests
"

Adam: "WOW... some day!"

Samantha: "And Trust me my dear Adam, I needed to see the future today, react to things before they happen, Set a Good Example to inspire my employees, Act responsibly as a Leader of the Company and finally report to the Board of Directors who's majority of them are Males looking at the Woman who should fall anytime..
"

Adam: "So what I experienced can be one small aspect of what a manager's have on his / her plate"

Samantha: "I'm not saying that what your manager did was wrong or right, I'm only implying that you need to look at her perceptive before you jump into Judging... maybe she is under pressure, being new in the role, and being a Woman in a 90% Males organization, and not being able to show her Stress..."

Samantha went on and on about the major differences between employee and Boss... Adam was very motivated and relieved by what Mrs. K has told him.

At the end of that evening, Adam thanked the Kays for their hospitality and grabbed the 2 books that Dr. K have given to him and went back to his Apartment.

Adam spent his weekend reading and reading, the books given to him by Dr. K, were almost telling his story... it was weird how some people think that they are exceptional, while what happen with them is actually pretty Normal.. and even more Predictable than they may think...

On Sunday evening, after he finished reading the 2 books, Adam opened his notebook and started writing...

What would you do?

Leadership is...

Adam woke up at 5:30 AM, Worked out on his treadmill at home, took a shower and dressed up for his presentation at FDT today;

"... and finally If you focus on shifting the paradigm of needs in communication for a traditional Chinese citizen from being the country who make things to people & switch it to become this: China, the country that will rule the world Soon and they are oath to understand the US business... you will have a chance!" Adam concluded his 1 hour and a half presentation...

Jill: "That's very impressive Adam, I like how you linked the last 2 points and where you wanted us to focus... Lila you should be proud of your Senior consultant!"

Jill, a middle-age executive who normally likes to throw a net over her customers until they are hooked, was a tough SVP to impress... so Adam felt flattered by her words.

Lila: "I told you not to worry"

Robin: "What about the plan on page 62; you said that we will need to introduce a new tablet-pc & join our efforts with a big software company when the market changes. I don't buy this, and I think that's not a good strategy; why did you include that Adam?"

Adam: "Well the mobile business itself is shifting, and the consumer behavior will reach to a phase when they will move from using their laptop to something different and that's not a phone, so all the marks & market studies say that Tablet will be the next best thing, and if you penetrate that market and didn't ride that wave, you'll be simply crushed."

Robin, the VP of Corporate Sales of FDT, did not like the tune of Adam's Voice.

Jill: "I think that Adam have a point, but our plans is NOT to produce another device nor to merge or do a venture with another company. So we'll just remove that part from the plan."

Adam was about to Blow up; He didn't find many solutions before he suggested that plan, and changing even a Piece of it, would simply screw it up.

"I don't think that would be a good idea" replied Adam.

Lila: "Adam is tiered from his last trip and I think after 2 hours talking about this, I believe we need to wrap up on this and agree to take Jill's Suggestion into action and change the plan"

Jill: "Adam… I want from you only one answer, do you recommend that we go for it?"

Adam: "Aaa… I don't think we neeee.." and just before he finishes his sentence Lila interrupted by saying

"Adam, you created this plan yourself, and you said that moving to china was a great option for FDT; so We need to take by Jill's Update and go for the plan"

Adam: "Frankly Jill, I don't think that's a good idea, especially if you're not planning into going into the tablet market."

Jill: "I didn't quite understand! Are you saying that we shouldn't go to China?"

"No" replied Adam quietly

Lila in a furious tune: "Adam, can you please talk to me in private; Jill & Robin will you excuse us for a second?"

Lila grabbed Adam from his arm and took him outside the meeting room and started yelling:

"Are you Out of your Mind!!!

What are you're trying to accomplish here??

We are NOT going to lose this deal... you go back there and fix that or else... I will fix that"

Adam: "You don't get it Lila, I'm doing what's best for the Customer not for us... there's no way they will make it into that market, especially if they skip my ONE recommendation."

Lila: "if we lose this deal, I will fire you... I'm giving you a direct request to Accept the change Jill wants to make to the plan and work to find a different solution which will make her suggestion succeed."

Adam and Lila went back to the now tensed meeting room,

Robin: "So? What's your final decision on that?"

Lila: "We will welcome Jill's Suggestion and Adam will find an alternative way to bring her suggestion to success."

Jill: "Adam, I need a direct answer from you, do I go to China and make money selling mobiles or no?"

Adam hesitated in answering, and took a long breath and replied to Jill...

"I'd rather you won't..."

Lila took a harsh look at Adam's Face with fire sparkling from her eyes, and grabbed her purse and left the meeting.

Adam tried to follow her, but she was quick to leave the scene, and in matter of less than 10 minutes he received a text message "You're Fired! I will send the stuff on your desk to the nearest branch of Burger king... Don't even bother to pass by the office."

This was a shocking moment for Adam, he didn't think that she would actually fire him, but it just happened.

It can be funny sometimes when everything around you start to collapse; in just one week, Adam ended a relationship, lost his dream job and found himself walking towards his apartment with really nothing much to lose.

That evening, Adam was hanging out with his friends at the SC Lounge bar.

"Cheer up Buddy, you're a bright man, you'll find a better job" Said Wess.

Adam: "You don't understand Wess, I was fired because I did the right thing for the customer's benefit... and my job is to see the future of my actions and the more BRIGHT this future will be, the better I am at my job... it's not a piece of software that you can 'Patch' and create Service Packs or fix Bugs later on like what you do."

Eddy: "What's done is done, tonight let's not look at what happened and let's try to find you a date."

Adam: "I Really, REALLY don't feel like it"

Eddy: "ok so let's just test some tactics tonight and have some fun. Do you see the brunette over there? She's looking at us non-stop."

Wess: "hehe, you're right Eddy she is!"

Adam: "you both are idiots... I'll be right back"

In less than 5 seconds, Adam went to the brunette and started chatting with her and wrote something on a small piece of paper and was back to the guys who were still in SHOCK from what just happened.

Adam: "Here's her number Eddy."

Eddy: "How the Hell did that happen???"

Adam: "Simple, when was the last time you saw a gorgeous girl sitting alone in a Bar?"

Eddy: "ummmmm... not much"

"Exactly, Beautiful girls don't risk going out to bars alone, they will attract un-wanted attention... unless she was actually a...."

Wess: "Prostitute!"

Adam smiled at Wess: "So your Logic does work after all"

"So having a 50-50 chance that she would be waiting for someone or waiting for a 'customer', I went there and asked for her a simple question."

Eddy & Wess at the same time: "and that simple question is......???"

Adam: "Are you expecting someone?"

Eddy & Wess: "Huh?"

Adam continued what happened:

"

She replied with a 'Yes'

How much time do I have before he gets here?

She replied, 'and why you're asking?'

Because I want to ask directions to the nearest library and I don't want him to perceive me as hitting on you

She replied, 'which book you want to check out from the library at this time'

And then I started lowering my voice till she leaned forward to hear what I was saying and I whispered 'How to make love all Night long'.

She then Laughed and replied to me 'how much are you willing to pay for that'

 I smiled and replied back 'Depending on the quality of the book'

And I ended up with her number that is for any of you to use."

Wess: "You're hilarious, what if she was waiting for her husband and he came and kicked your ass"

Adam: "the key is to adapt your body language in a safe way"

Eddy: "adapt our body language?"

Adam: "when you approach a girl, you need to have a specific body language that would be GLIMPSY... meaning that it would adapt to the situation."

"I went there, but I wasn't 100% facing her, my body was forward, and only my head was towards her... when the conversation has heated, I easily adapted to the situation."

Eddy: "this way if her BF jumped in, you will simply turn your head and continue ordering a drink without attracting much attention to the situation; Nice Tactic."

Wess: "I don't buy this, you were just lucky; things wouldn't have worked out if she was a nice girl and if she was in a group."

Adam: "Allow me to demonstrate it... but we will need to move to a different place."

The 3 guys, went out from the pub to a club nearby, and before they get in, Adam pushed some rules first.

As soon as they went into the club, they spotted a group of friends, 2 guys and 4 girls sitting and laughing; Adam threw in the spotting signal and they went into that direction and sat at the table near them.

Adam noticed that one of the guys was heading to the bathroom, and he followed him.

"It's a crazy world, did you see the fight that happened outside?" Adam said to the guy who was washing his hands.

Jimmy: "Fight? No I haven't... What was it about?"

Adam: "Apparently a girl spotted her boyfriend cheating on her with another, so she was literally destroying his car and kicking his ass."

Jimmy: "Wow, well girls can unleash the dragon sometimes..."

Adam: "There's nothing more interesting than a Cat's Fight, apparently her boyfriend's other girlfriend arrived and went into a fighting mode with her... so the scene got more interesting."

Jimmy: "SWEET!! What happened next??"

Adam: "do you want us to order a drink? We're in the bathroom!!!"

Jimmy smiled: "Ah sorry..."

Adam went inside the bathroom and Jimmy went back to his friends and he didn't know that Adam & the guys were sitting right next to them.

Jimmy was back to his friends, and initiated the story to his group...

In few more minutes, while Adam was watching from a far, when he sensed that the enthusiasm heated from the story, he started walking back...

"Ah There you are, I was just talking to my friends about your story..." Jimmy said to Adam.

Adam looked at the ladies in the group while Still Standing: "Well, let me ask you a quick question... If a guy cheated on you... What would you do to him?"

The girls started giggling and started throwing random answers and before they continue their chat.

Adam: "I must leave you here to discuss it over, I'm here with some of my friends so I'll check on you later."

Adam sat with Eddy and Wess and gave them his Back.

Wess: "ok so now what?"

Eddy: "The girls are checking you out from behind..."

Adam: "Wait... it will happen, let's continue with the plan."

Few minutes later, laughter raised from Adam's Table... it seems the guys were having a great time catching up.

What actually happened was that Adam threw in a teaser on an unfinished conversation, and then switched to another table, explicitly showing that he and his friends are here to catch up and have a good time rather than picking up girls.

Few more minutes, Jimmy turned his back and asked Adam and his friends to join the tables and join in.

The hottest girl in the group was Rola, she was trying to look careless and un-interested in the conversation.

Adam: "Now I'm going to give you girls 3 tools to choose one from and let your vivid imagination guide your way on what to do next with the guy after he is kidnaped and tied up blind-folded to a chair at your house."

Adam was intentionally not paying too much attention to Rola, and instead was directing the conversation to her other friends.

"That's Lame... I don't know why we're even discussing this" Said Rola.

"Is she for real?" Adam smiled while barely directing a full look to Rola and continued his talk.

Adam: "ok girls, now that each of you has an answer... hear out my following question... If your, Now Ex, spoke a shocking sentence like... 'I did it because you drove me to it'... 'it was because all of your actions'... 'You Took me for granted for too long'... What would your reaction be?"

The girls of the group were in a SHOCK mode, they took a silent moment as if 'the pretending' actually happened to them.

Adam took advantage of the silent mode to look and eye to eye towards Rola and asks her...

"Nice Nails. Are they for real?"

"mmmmm, well they are... Not" Rola answered while she didn't notice that Adam was trying to put her down.

Adam then said while wearing a funny smile: "Oh [paused]. Well, I guess they still look good" and turned his back to Rola and continued talking to the girls.

The conversation went on and on here and there... And in a fraction of a second Wess said: "Oh Boy..."

Eddy turned and got little more shocked... "Oh Boy!!"

Something unexpected just happened. Natasha, Adam's Ex, just went into the Club with another guy.

Adam who didn't notice what just happened and was preparing to hit the R in Rola, was having a laugh when he just noticed a VERY familiar face staring at him from across the hall.

The music stopped, everything stopped moving, Adam could almost hear his heart beating... What just happened was exactly what was missing in making his day even BETTER.

Natasha was looking gorgeous as usual, her long black hair shining on the spotting lights of the club; she had incredible eyes and at that moment they were focusing on only one thing... ADAM.

Eddy: "It's getting late; let's just call off the day"

Wess: "Yeah I'm tiered too... Adam let's go!"

"NO... We JUST Got here" Adam replied fearlessly.

Then the guys who were into the club to experience some Venusian tactics are now prepared to experience the "CLASH OF THE TITANS".

"If you would excuse me... I'll be right back" Adam said while standing up, pointing his feet in the direction of Natasha and not even waiting for an approval from anyone.

"Hey..." Said Adam to Natasha.

Natasha Sarcastically "Well Well Well, Look who's here.."

Natasha was not by herself at the Bar, Gary-The-Midnight-Runner was next to her. Gary was a known Boxer and he was looking for a chance to impress Natasha so he jumped into the scene.

"Any problem Nat? Is this guy bothering you".

Adam: "Now that you mentioned it... it's almost Midnight, why don't you go RUN somewhere while Adults talk."

Gary was about to grab his Fist and Teach Adam a lesson in manners but he didn't.

Natasha: "Seriously Adam, why are you even here?"

"I'm here to order a Drink...." And just before Adam finishes his sentence...

"For me..." Rola said while magically stepping into the conversation

Natasha: "And why didn't you order your own drink Senorita" while raising the AAAh in Senorita.

Rola: "Simply Because you're in between me and my Marguritaaaaa"

Adam was in an awkward moment; Rola Gently grabbed his arm and told him, "Let's Dance!"

Apparently Rola was an angel sent from heaven to be at that place at that particular time and the story got more interesting.

Adam and Rola started Dancing and then Rola whispered in his ear.

"You owe me one, story teller"

Adam, while dancing, grabbed her waist turned her entire body to face Natasha and pulled her back toward his chest and whispered in her ear... "No I don't"

Natasha who was burning from Jealousy, approached Gary intimately and started almost licking his ear while talking.

Wess, Eddy and the group were about to order pop-corn as the scene before them was better than watching a movie.

The music kept getting louder, Adam realized that he's playing a game doomed for failure, since he didn't have intentions towards Rola; So, he simply continued dancing and sent a signal to his buddies to take care of the check and meet him outside.

"Listen Rola, I don't like to owe anyone... That's why I'm going to return the favor right now..." Adam pulled a small paper from him pocket wrote something on it and slipped it in Rola's Tight Jeans,

"I'll be back..." he said while he disappeared in the crowd.

Rola waited few minutes and then opened the note that said 'Asta La Vista, Baby...'

Adam left the club and got back home... He was furious from one LONG DAY...

He took his Notebook as if has not been writing for a long time, wrote one Sentence only and closed it and went to sleep...

Born to be Alive

The Pyramid of Needs

Adam was jobless, but he was not really looking for a Job, he simply needed to take some time off before he take a decision on where he wanted to be next.

Over the following week, he cleaned his apartment, threw away lots of stuff and deleted several photos and messages from his phone... He has finally finished procrastinating on his own life.

Since now Adam had more time on his hands, he started visiting the Kays more often and helping them in some housework and research.

One day, Eric asked Adam to take him out to lunch and of course Adam accepted and they both went to a very nice park near the Lake.

"What's wrong with life Dr. K, every time you accomplish something, something else has to rise and you will have to start all over again...? As if the pressure never ends in the cycle of Life!" Adam said while pushing Eric's Wheelchair in the park.

Eric: "There's nothing *wrong* with Life, you just don't realize that you're *moving* stages or levels..."

Adam: "Moving levels? You mean like a video-game?"

Eric: "Precisely!"

"You see when you're playing a video game, the first few times you play, the first few levels would seem hard... but after a while you can easily finish them and move to the next ones who then would seem hard and so on."

"Let me ask you this Adam, have you ever felt that after you finished level 3 in a game, you wanted to go back to level 2 or move to level 4?"

Adam: "mmmmm.... Of course skip to the Next level"

Eric: "That exactly is the cycle of Life... We Live to Skip to the next levels... Oh there it is, let's have lunch here"

After having a delicious lunch, they ordered tea and Eric continued his point...

"In the 50s a talented and bright psychologist who brought what is now used in the foundation of Sales & Marketing, Abraham Maslow set the stage of what is now called, the *Hierarchy of Needs*.

I do quote from his writings that being a human being – in terms of being born to the human species – must be defined also in terms of 'becoming' a human being. In this sense a baby is only potentially a human being, and must grow into humanness.

And that is why people feel that life is changing for them when they get older, and some things starts to matter more while other things start to matter... *LESS*

Now Maslow designed the hierarchy of becoming a human being as a pyramid with the following three layers from the ground up: the Physiological – Air, food and water – the psychological – Safety, Love and Self-esteem – and, finally, self-actualization. "

Adam: "interesting, so that applies to all humans?"

Eric: "Indeed! You won't search for self-esteem and the need to feel accomplished if you're hungry or if you feel un-safe, in fact messing around the order of the needs and trying to accomplish something before the other will only lead to more damage than having the original need not fulfilled..."

Adam: "Just like if someone tries to put orange juice in his car tank instead of fuel"

Eric: "Exactly! It's a funny example, but true. Now needs and wants are two different things, although very related but different."

Adam: "Why is that Dr. K?"

Eric: "Wants are normally calculated on the conscious level... so you would say I Want to do this or that... While needs are calculated on a more sub-conscious level."

"But one knows when he needs to eat... Am I Right?" said Adam

Eric: "Well, you are partially right, because the lower part of the pyramid is more obvious to identify... while when you go higher in the pyramid it becomes tricky to identify those needs... Have you ever woke up one day saying: 'I need a PHD?' it's easier to know what you want when you identify that you need it and especially WHEN you need it."

Adam: "I'm lost here, can you please let me know where you're going with this?"

Eric laughed and sipped his tea and took a long view of the lake and then continued:

"The Magic of the human Life is that it's unpredictable, not everyone grows up to become a doctor, not everyone wants to be super rich or wants to wake up early and go for a 5 km run, do you think lots of people from your neighborhood think about the necessity to cure hunger in some countries in Africa?

The answer is no, people have different needs... But hear this, unfortunately lots of them would happily accept to satisfy a higher need if it was given to them effortlessly."

Adam: "You Lost me again…"

Eric: "Ok let me ask you something… would you like to be the person who would cure a serious disease like cancer and save millions of people worldwide and have your name craved in history? Would you want that?"

Adam: "Off Course!"

Eric: "Are you willing to isolate and dedicate yourself to research for like 20 years with barely any social life and you may or may not have a wealthy life or even a higher chance of succeeding in your quest?"

Adam: "Well… "

Eric: "How about I asked you this even simpler question...

If you were a worker who makes 500$ per month, would you spend your one month salary on buying an expensive Pen?
"

Adam: "I guess not..."

Eric: "Now how about I gave you the 500$... would you go and buy an expensive pen?"

Adam: "I don't think so too... I would use it for something else that has more priority"

Eric: "ok one last thing, what if I GAVE you an expensive pen, would you accept it?"

Adam: "I certainly would."

Eric: "Which lead me to the conclusion... Most people want to go to heaven, but they are not ready to die for it... they want to earn lots of money but they're not ready to work hard for that or even wait for that to happen... and so on"

Adam: "And how does that applies in Relationships"

Eric: "I thought you would ask that!

Relationships fall into the category of psychological needs that include Love & Belongingness in addition to Esteem Needs, but also to note that 'Sex' itself is a physiological need which is part of the lower categories of the pyramid."

Adam: "Now that's cool! Are you saying that a person needs Sex before Love???"

Eric: "Yeah it's funny, but true. Let's replace the term 'Sex' with 'Physical Attraction' so I don't feel weird talking to you about this subject"

Adam: "ok I promise I won't make this subject turns into something inappropriate to discuss..."

Eric: "you got what I meant... now back to subject"

Adam: "Please proceed!"

Eric: "in some conservative cultures, and when you're also less experienced, more relationship fails because of the confusion between Love & Physical attraction...

You see, some *think* that they are in love with someone, while they are simply *physically attracted* to them, so when that need is fulfilled, if there was no other offers on the table between both... things will become more off than on and the relationship will start to crack down."

Adam: "I can't imagine myself with someone I'm not physically attracted to... "

Eric: "Well the problem sometimes rise from trying to substitute certain needs with others... so per example trying to eat more chocolate while your body needs vegetables; I mean haven't you gone to a restaurant one day and started drinking more soft-drinks and still feeling thirsty? While one glass of water would've been enough!"

Adam: "That happened couple of times, yes"

Eric: "And it happens thousands of times with millions of people around the globe. And that alone brings headache, stress and disappointment.

There are so many people who THINK that they have a specific need at the time, while in reality they don't. The need they are trying to satisfy is misplaced. And that's my dear Adam is your answer to your question about what's wrong with Life!"

Dr. Kays & Adam kept talking & discussing several psychology theories inside out, the conversation was very deep and Adam had new horizons that got widened from the subject itself.

"Now let us play a game" said Dr. Kays to Adam

Adam: "A Game?"

Eric: "is it Tuesday or Wednesday?"

Adam: "It's Tuesday, Next question..."

Eric: "have you ever gone to a Speed dating activity before?"

Adam then looked up in the sky and started visualizing a long line of strippers going across him and then woke up: "Let's say I've done something similar several years ago; but why are you asking?"

Eric: "Because I have an activity for us to do; I hope you don't have any appointments later on."

Adam laughed and knew that he was about to have fun while learning something new: "What are you up to?"

Eric: "Let's have some fun while helping other people; today is 'Good Psychologist's Tuesday' at the 12th street community center"

Adam: "Interesting... Waiter may we have the check please!"

'Good Psychologist's Tuesday' was an interesting initiative held every 3rd

Tuesday of the month at some of the city's community centers where volunteer psychologists interact in a speed consultation format with other individuals trying to advise them anonymously.

The process was simple; there were around 30 tables, and on each will be a masked psychologist, and the individuals will each have 10 minutes with the psychologist and then the bell will ring and a rotation will happen to allow the individuals to benefit from another consultation.

There were 3 types of Masks: the Psychologist, The Male and the Female. This way the psychologists can be separated from the individuals and they will immediately know if the person facing them is a Male or a Female; No other information is to be shared.

Dr. Kays wanted to prove to Adam that most of today's problems are simply the miss-placement of the levels of the pyramid of needs. He coached him on the way on what he should focus in this "mission" to be successful.

Adam placed the Psychologist Mask on his face, and went and got installed on Table number 7 while Dr. Kays went to the table number 20 which was almost facing Adam's from the other part of the room.

Then one of the organizers spoke in a loud voice:

"Greetings Psychologists!

Remember the one rule we have... Anonymity of Identities is Sacred and so is our Mission to help others beyond border. Enjoy your time and respect the time!"

The doors were opened and a group of masked men and women entered the room and each sat on a table.

There was a large timer clock in the middle of the room and a small one on each of the tables.

A Big Bell rang announcing the start of the Speed Consultation.

Adam was very excited, it was a new experience for him and he was sure that it will bring him lots of value, in addition to simply helping others as much as possible.

Man: "I hate my job, I'm not appreciated, I'm under-paid, I don't have a purpose in life and my social life is heading nowhere, what should I do doctor?"

Adam smiled when he heard the word *Doctor* and asked the masked man.

"How do you spend your time?"

Man: "I clean streets; I'm a street sweeper"

Adam: "what time you start working?"

Man: "5 AM every day, and I finish cleaning by 8 AM before people start going to their work, then I restart by 8 PM till 11PM"

Adam: "and what do you do in between"
Man: "Nothing much, I sometimes sleep, or watch TV, or hang out with some friends"

Adam: "do you have a family?"
Man: "yes I'm married with 2 kids"

Adam: "do you make enough money to have a decent living with your family?"

Man: "Decent yes, luxury No"
Adam: "and what's your definition of luxury?"

Man: "To live easily, to have all the toys your heart desires, and to be appreciated by others."

Adam: "what do you say about someone who spends most of his day doing WHATEVER he wanted, watching TV, Hanging out, have time for his children and his wife, and yet doing a very important role in society?"

Man: "He's one lucky person."
Adam: "I was talking about you Sir... take a good look at yourself and you will realize that the only person between you and seeing what you already have is your perception and comparing yourself to others; you see not many have the luxury of living the way you do, so try to take a step back and appreciate what you have before you start looking at others and devaluating what you already have."

You couldn't see the facial reactions on each because of the masks, but you could hear from the silence that was heard despite the voices around that the sentence touched the Man and just before he could reply back, the bell rang and it was time to switch.

A woman sat before Adam, She obviously had an over-weight issue, so He was almost predicting what she was going to say...

Woman: "Hello, I'm a Kindergarten teacher... I have been doing that since forever now and recently I have issues with the kids I teach. Also my colleagues started avoiding me and my superiors are thinking of letting me go. What do I do?"

Adam: "Are you Married Ms.?"
Woman: "I have a boyfriend."

Adam: "how long have you been with him if I may ask?"
Woman: "2 and half years this September"

Adam: "How's your relationship with him?"

Woman: "Excuse me Mr., but why are you asking me about my personal life while I'm stating that my issue is with my professional life?"

Adam: "You still have 7 minutes, are you sure you want to discuss the 'why'?"
Woman: "Ok, whatever... Well things with me and my Boyfriend was going well, but let's say recently I had a physical condition that gave me some extra weight, things are not going as great as it once was."

Adam: "And how does that make you feel?"
Woman: "Of course I'm destroyed... I love Jerry with everything I have, and it kills me to see him becoming less interested. As if I have enough troubles in my life as it is right now!"

Adam: "And you think that the main cause is your weight?"
Woman: "I hope not!"

Adam: "let me ask you this question, if you're to choose to buy from 2 sales persons; where both are equally competent, but one person is cheerful and the other one is always depressed... Which one would you choose?"

Woman: "Of course, the Cheerful person."

Adam: "And why is that?"
Woman: "Because life is too short for negative people and depressed ones; we have enough in our lives to tolerate negativity."

Adam: "Kids can sense the negativity from across the room, they would cry even another kid started crying and they feel the empathy more than you think... and they are simply reacting to you.

Your colleagues feel the depressing mode you have, and took the same decision you made with the cheerful salesperson. Your management saw your recent behavior affecting your performance and almost doing a bigger impact on the kids and therefore they are thinking of replacing you.

And finally, your BF Loves YOU and Only YOU very much, however you're not *YOU* lately... which is more than a reason for him to act this way so All you need to do is to look back at your life and see what's missing... and the solution would be easier than you think."

The Loud sound of silence stroke again... Only to be interrupted by the sound of the Bell.

Masked men & women kept on rotating in the *Speedotherapy* game and it lasted for another hour and so.

Adam was filled with Joy because he felt like helping others, while not revealing his identity and with no pressure of the real therapy, because everyone treats it as a non-formal way of helping and more of an Land an listening ear than to actually help.

Adam thanks Dr. Kays for the lovely day, as he learned more in that day than he did in years and years.

Adam went back to his place, opening his notebook and started writing, and writing till almost morning light. Then he fell into a deep sleep knowing that he doesn't have to be anywhere that day.

Fake it till you Make it

Cash or Credit?

48 days later, FDT announced that their plans to go with China failed and that they will shift strategies.

Adam read that in the news, he had mixed feelings about it, but was little satisfied since he lost his job because of that deal;

He then received an invitation for a meeting at FDT, but this time by Daren, the Senior Vice President of Operations at A4, the Holding Company that owns FDT and around 36 others.

Adam was surprised that anyone from A4 knew him, and also that the timing was a bit surprising. Nevertheless, he was ready for any type of meetings since he always had integrity "built-in" all his life, especially when he dealt with their accounts.

Friday morning, 8:51 AM, Adam was sitting in the lobby of one of the biggest & most powerful corporations in the nation.

A Lady welcomed him into the big meeting room, where she asked him to wait.

At 9:00 AM sharp, four executives entered the room, Adam recognized only one, SVP Jill from FDT.

Jill: "Good to see you again Adam, Allow me to introduce you to Daren, SVP of A4 who personally caters for acquisitions, business transformation and expansions."

Adam: "It's a pleasure meeting you Sir..."

Daren: "Simone, my business manager and Jeffery Director of Corporate strategy across all A4's companies will be with us today."

Adam: "Simone, Jeffery, good day…"

Daren: "The Reason why we invited you to this meeting, Adam, is to get to know you and to see if there are opportunities for us to collaborate."

Adam was a little confused… He tough he will be meeting with lawyers and facing law suits etc…

"I thank you for inviting to the meeting, I'm curious to learn more about the invitation *reason*." Replied Adam

Daren: "I was not happy in the past 2 months on how the operations were running in FDT, and obviously you knew about our plans' failure in China. That's embarrassing!!"

Simone: "After evaluating the entire process to find out the reason of the failure, Jill's report pointed several things from your statements that, may or may not, would've saved the situation if executed."

Jill: "In Brief Adam, you did have a point that we neglected and that contributed in the loss of a huge investment from our end."

Adam, with a smile: "What is done is done, no hard feelings."

Daren: "We could use a visionary consultant like you in A4. Are you as good in solving problems as you are in foreseeing them?"

Adam: "There's only one way to find out..."

Jill: "How is that?"

Adam: "Jeffery knows how..."

Jeffery, who hasn't said a word since the beginning of the meeting, was surprised to be mentioned by Adam in that context.

"I Beg your pardon?" said Jeffery

Adam: "I'm sure you were invited to this meeting for a reason. And based on my researches, I learned that you recently accepted an offer outside of A4 and you're now in your notice period, so that leads to one of either conclusions, 1) I'm here to potentially take your place."

Jeffery: "and what's number 2?"

"There is no Number 2." Adam replied while smiling diabolically.

Simone, Speaking in Spanish to Daren: *"que es más inteligente de lo que aparenta"*

(Translated to: "He's Smarter than he looks")

Daren replied in Spanish: *"No estoy muy seguro, él ha estado aquí"*

(Translated to: "I'm not sure, he's been here 10 minutes")

Daren Continued in Russian: *"YA dumayu, chto eto budetinteresnaya vstrecha"*

(Translated to: "I think it's going to be an interesting meeting")

Simone Smiled and replied back in Russian: *"da"*
(Translated to "Yeah")

Adam smiled and looked at Simone,

"eto nevezhlivo obrashchat'sya k sebe kak "on" ... a ya nastoyashchiĭ "

(Translated in English from Russian: "it's impolite to refer to myself as 'he'.... While I'm still here")

He then looked at Daren and continued in Spanish: *"y me ha estado aquí 13 minutos..."*

(Translated: "And I've been here 13 minutes...")

All four executives were astonished by what just happened, Adam who have been continuously improving his knowledge and skills over the past 5 years, has learned several languages in addition to reading many books.

Daren, acting as if nothing has just happened: "Let's not get ahead of ourselves here, we have an interesting task for you, and if you managed to pull it together, we would like to offer you a job in A4."

Daren continued: "One of our companies, P Plus Inc., is losing market share, most of the staff is demotivated and we're tired of injecting funds and resources in it without notable results. And we want to turn things around."

Adam: "P Plus is a good company, it's sad that they are facing issues. Now let me ask you this, if I managed to turn things around... What are you willing to offer me?"

Simone: "Jeffery's position."

Adam: "But he's moving in like 2 months from now and I never accomplished a job like this in less than 6 months."

Daren: "in 6 months P Plus is going to burn down. So you have 3 months to start getting results or things will become more complicated for the 400 employees working there."

Adam: "and what makes you think that I would accept the task?"

Jill: "Because you will be making a good deal of Money, a Success Story not to mention to securing a dream job for an ambitious person such as yourself."

Adam: "you have no idea of my ambition… I will accept the task in two conditions."

Daren: "Which are?"

Adam: "1) I will be Acting-Managing Director to P Plus which will give me authority to make changes internally versus working as a consultant and giving advices."

Daren: "ok. What's Number two?" (And here he was smiling and looking at Jeffery)

Adam smiled back: "Number Two is that if I manage to stop the negative growth, and turned things around in 3 months, you will have me appointed CEO of P Plus."

Jeffery: "That's obscured, Daren you can't be possibly accepting this? He doesn't have the profile or the necessary experience to become CEO."

Daren: "You do realize that P Plus has a relatively big structure to be handled by an inexperienced manager and that you will face lots of challenges fitting in with the current board of directors, who are all double your age and very tough to handle."

Adam Stood up, grabbed his things, and replied while smiling.

"So I would manage to save 400 Jobs, a big investment, and protect A4 from looking bad before its shareholders after a big Public embarrassment from FDT's China failure... But I won't fit to lead the Company.

Jill, Simone, Gentlemen... Good Day!"

Adam started walking toward the door, but stopped when Daren started Clapping at him.

"Bueono Adam... Ochen' khoroshiĭ"

(Translated: "Good Adam, Very Good")

Daren: "You grabbed my attention, I'm 'temporary' impressed; if you could pull this together, you would demonstrate your effectiveness in a task even the best people in our organization failed in fulfilling... So I don't see a reason why shouldn't we appoint you CEO afterwards."

Jill: "I do think you're too young for the ambition you have, but I have to say that I was wrong before not to trust your perspective, so I vote yes for granting your conditions."

Jeffery: "That's quite a show you had there Adam; unfortunately this is real life, you can't gamble with people's future just to prove you're somebody... I'm moving out anyway, so I'm happy that I won't be there to witness your big failure... I'll vote yes just for the sake of entertainment."

Daren: "Then it's set, Simone will coordinate with you all the details."

The meeting was closed, and Adam was on his way back home in a gamma state of mind, his mind was swimming in a climax of chemicals while he still didn't believe what just happened.

...Few hours later at the "Supremo Coffee Shop".

"YOU DID WHAT??" Said NOUR

Adam: "Oh Yes, that's exactly what happened"

Nour: "You're nuts, do you realize that you're about to flush 400 jobs in the toilet if you fail"

Adam: "you're very supportive Nour, anyone told you that before?"

Nour: "I'm only speaking common sense... You don't have the expertise, you don't even have a job and you were certainly bluffing... How did you do that?"

Adam: "All the Good people are taken, same thing applies to talents... If you're good in what you do and you're sitting at home finding difficulties looking for a job... people will presume that you're not what you claim to be..."

Nour: "But that's the reality, you're just a simple person with no job, no girlfriend and mainly no money... Again Adam, how did you gamble to get a good Job as a Director in one of the biggest corporations in the region and chased a 1 chance in a 1000; They could've refused your request and you ended up with nothing..."

Adam: "Just like the actors of the movies, you build yourself based on the end result you want to achieve...

And People will like it eventually and will believe in you."

Nour: "One Word... ENVY!!!"

The weekend was gone in minutes, Adam was about to start the Journey that would change his life... Forever.

Monday morning, 7:55 AM, Adam was at the elevator of P Plus INC; he saw a young man holding a box of papers who reminded him of his early beginnings.

"Which floor is management?" said Adam to the young man.

"15th, are you applying for a job here?" replied the young man.

Adam: "Sort of..."

Young Man: "I don't advise you to do so, from the outside P Plus looks like a great company, but when you go inside, the Big PLUS sign turns into a Big MINUS"

Adam: "Interesting to know... Does everyone share your conclusion?"

Young Man: "Everyone except the folks in the 15th floor... they never listen to the demands of the rest of us, and only focus on the sales and the revenue... It's not fun working here anymore... but what shall we do, it's better than the alternative."

Adam: "And What is the alternative?"

Young Man: "feeling pathetic... and NOT getting paid."

Adam: "I'll keep that in mind... it was a nice chat Mr. ...?"

"Jamal..." Said the Young Man

Adam: "Great talking to you Jamal"

Jamal: "and what's your name sir?"

Adam: "for now... I'm your new friend"

Adam reached the 15th floor, and was greeted by Simone who was waiting for his arrival.

Simone: "buenos días Adam" (Good Morning in Spanish)

Adam: "Bonjour Simone!" (Good Morning in French)

Simone: "You are full of surprises Adam, how many languages do you know?"

Adam: "What time does everyone arrive in here?"

Simone: "P Plus Starts at 9:00 AM, but most of the management starts arriving at 9:30 and some arrives at 10:00"

Adam: "mmmm.... Interesting!"

Simone: "Ah Well, things used to be much more active as I heard, but recently everyone is demotivated from the situation and I believe that... "

Adam interrupted: "Simone, beside you, Daren, Jill and Jeffery, who else knows about our deal?"

Simone: "Well practically no one, things happened quickly and it was already a weekend so we were going to wait until today to announce it to the board and to the management, Basically introducing you to them directly today."

Adam: "Can I ask you for a favor?"

Simone was a little confused... "A Favor?"

Adam: "Yes, can you please lay low on our arrangement and schedule me an interview for a Marketing position."

Simone: "Look Adam, I admired your ambition on Friday but if you think that this is some sort of a game, please take this seriously."

Adam: "I'm not joking... Trust me on this... just play along until noon."

Simone: "Ok, I really hope you're aware of what you're doing".

Simone made a call with the HR Manager of P Plus, and got Adam an interview at 10:00 AM.

"You can come and wait with me in Sergey's office" Said Simone.

Adam: "Who's Sergey?"

Simone: "He's the ex-COO of the company, he got fired last month."

Adam: "What about the CEO... Who's That?"

Simone: "Gavin? He's on a vacation; he should be back next week."

Adam: "How long has he been on a Vacation?"

Simone: "His Granddaughter got married recently, so he went with his family in a celebration sailing cruise to Europe. That was Last month"

Adam, talking to himself: "This just keeps getting better and better"

At 9:00 AM, there was no one still in the floor, except for the receptionist, Adam and Simone.

9:30 AM, The CFO of the company arrived, didn't bother greeting anyone, just continued towards his office and closed the door.

9:40 AM everyone else started arriving. And within 20 minutes, the floor was filled with what it looks like, "Expensive Executives".

It was already 10:00 AM; Simone has left based on her agreement with Adam to be back at noon.

"Excuse me miss, I have an appointment Scheduled at 10:00 AM with HR for a Marketing position; it's

10:01 AM already and I haven't been called for. Can you please help me out locating the interviewer?" Said Adam to the Receptionist

Receptionist: "You've been here since a while young man; Benjamin haven't arrived yet, and he's the HR Manager. I'll make sure to call for you as soon as he's here."

Adam: "Thank you miss…"

10:15 AM Benjamin arrived to the office; he spoke briefly with the receptionist who was pointing at Adam. Benjamin walked towards Adam Holding his coffee and his briefcase,

"I don't like to conduct interviews in early mornings; But I'm going to make an exception for you Kid, since you've been recommended by Simone. Step into my office. "

Adam: "Good Morning to you too sir."

Before Benjamin arrived, Adam thought he would be expecting an old man with few years before retirement, he was surprised to notice that Benjamin was relatively young, maybe in his late 30s, but apparently have an ego bigger than his rounded belly....

"... And when I told her I don't want the discount on my New Audi she was surprised... can you imagine! But I really didn't care about the discount, they can keep it... I have money, I'm paying 80,000 Dollars, and I wasn't very happy with the color." Benjamin was talking and talking for around 20 minutes about his Glory days.

Adam: "So tell me about the position in PPlus and why should I work here?"

Benjamin: "To tell you the truth Kid, it's not WHAT you know... it's WHO you know that would make you survive in this mad world, and obviously you KNOW someone... So you can start immediately, Blend into the existing System, lay your head low and do your best... that's how things are done around here... "

Adam was SHOCKED from hearing such a corrupted transparency... He replied back with a smile that says (I get it)...

"I've heard things were not going well in here... how are you guys surviving?"

Benjamin: "There's a truth in what you're saying... Well things were not always like that... There was a time when the Company was inspired by a great leader... The Former CEO... SAM, he had a great vision, was down to earth and he was always leading by example... Everyone loved working under his leadership... But sometimes bad things happen to good people... He had a fight with the Board of directors, after he got sick of them getting paid with practically no return on their expenses... He did however clean things out, but later he resigned and moved on to work for one of the biggest companies in the world in a senior position."

Adam: "so what happens now? When can I start?"

Benjamin: "You will need to have a Chat with the CFO regarding your package and stuff..."

Adam: "Ok... How's that going to happen?"

Benjamin: "Oh, his Office is right across the hall... Just feel free to go and go straight in, I'll call him on the phone to let him know you're coming."

Adam was not surprised that the CFO of the company is in an "available" mode to the rest of the company, even if it's just a perception; So, he stood up, shacked hands with Benjamin and started walking slowly toward the office of the CFO.

It was almost 11:30 AM, and as he was walking he noticed the desk of the CFO's assistant is empty and the door of the office is closed, but not locked.

He knocked gently, and waited... then he knocked again... and at that time he heard some laughs from inside the office and a female voice calling sentences that are unlikely to be work related.

He opened the door and looked carefully to see the CFO obviously was trying to find a penny under his assistant's BRA while she is sitting on his desk with her legs spread!

Adam didn't bother to enter the room, and just closed the door and walked away to call Simone.

Simone (on the phone with Adam): "How's your Theatrical Play going?"

Adam: "it went from a Cartoon to a PG-13 and finally to an R / 18+ and it's not even Noon YET... I Need something from you, let us meet here at 2 PM"

Simone: "But you said Noon... "

Adam: "I know what I said, I knew what I wanted from the TOP, and I need to go down a bit to see how messed up the situation is... 2 PM please on the 15th floor"

Simone: "Ok... You got it!"

Adam walked towards the receptionist, and started chatting with her.

"Miss, can I ask you for a small thing... I just got hired here and I need to know my way around, can you please call a person called JAMAL to escort me to see more of the company?"

Receptionist: "Of course sire, and may I congratulate you on your new position... In which department exactly?"

Adam: "Sales & Marketing... and Thank you very much for your kind words."

The receptionist, who was very nice and kind, called Jamal to come up & escort Adam to see more of the company.

While waiting, Adam smiled at the receptionist and asked her a direct question...

"How long have you been in the company Miss?"

Receptionist: "Almost 5 years now... "

Adam: "Wow, that's a while... so you must know your way around very well..."

Receptionist: "Yes I started as a part time job to pay for my Masters and when I graduated, they promised to promote me to a good position and I've been waiting for that since at least 2 years now"

Adam: "You studied what exactly?"

Receptionist: "I have a Bachelor in Business Management and then I continued my MBA in Corporate Finance."

Adam was SHOCKED from what he was hearing!!!

"I'm sorry to be interfering Miss, but if I may ask... What are you still doing here as a Receptionist!!!"

"There's lots of experience I'm gaining" replied the receptionist.

Adam was confused... "I beg your pardon?"

Receptionist: "Well you obviously met our CFO, and his 'Elegant' Assistant Vicky... So ever since they knew that I was a Finance Major, and since they get into much 'closed meetings' so they give me extended tasks that includes Vicky's duties and some projects from the CFO's office and I'm ok with that because I get exposed to great things. And I get to leave early with no responsibility!"

Adam: "Aha"

Jamal arrived and smiled and greeted Adam: "Hello new friend!! Any luck?"

Adam (silently): "You have no idea..."

Jamal escorted the young Adam down to the 7th floor to the Sales & Marketing department.

To his surprise, the floor seemed like a 180 degrees different from the 15th, as if they traveled from Hawaii to New York... from Vacation Mood to a Serious Work Mood.

Jamal showed him around, but everyone seemed really busy jumping all over the place, so he only pointed Adam toward a young lady that should be working with him.

"You must be new here, no one bothers to send us the Memo anymore; I'm Faten... Why don't you come with me, we're going to have a meeting with the team in like 10 minutes."

"I'm Adam, Nice to meet you Faten"

They both went into a meeting room, where there were already around 7 people chatting aggressively and pointing towards the white board and some were really nervous.

Faten: "Hey everyone, this is Adam and he's New here"

Adam: "Hi Everyone, I'm glad to be...." But he couldn't get to finish his sentence where the meeting started and everyone practically shifted focus.

A relatively young male was leading the meeting.

Eduardo: "Hey Folks, again I don't have some good news from upstairs, sometimes I just feel that they don't read the reports we send... So again our request for more Funding on the KANATA project was declined for the reason that the company is having cash-flow issues and they prefer to shift the funding toward something with immediate returns"

Faten: "This project can save the company or at least place us toward a leading position whcre we could be back on track"

Rudy: "There's a long shot that I can make with KANATA. But it's a bit risky, if we could somehow crunch some of their numbers that we could gather publicly and integrate the simulation of our solution into their current losses, and show them the ROI (Return on Investment) by linking the cost to the savings... We may have a shot there, but I need your support team"

Adam was shocked seeing a Team Uniting and collaborating, toward a common goal while their management was the actual wall between them and success.

He kept quite watching a REAL Team at work and enjoying the debates; when the meeting was done, he asked Faten if Eduardo was the Manager of the unit, she laughed and replied… Nope, it was Rudy, but he empowered us in a big way that we all feel equally accountable and united.

Adam went out of the meeting feeling very proud and optimistic about the future of the company that its employees have such a high caliber.

Adam pressed couple of buttons on his mobile: "Hi Simone, I'm ready for you… can you meet me at the 15th floor"

20 minutes later, Simone and Adam were sitting at Sergey's office.

Adam: "This Company needs to *turn up-side-down...* and I mean that Literally!

The people who work downstairs need to be in management and those in management need to be downstairs or even kicked out of the company. "

And then Adam continued explaining to Simone what was actually happening in the company; and after around 20 minutes of talking and debating...

Simone: "Adam, are you sure you want to do that?"

Adam: "Very!"

Simone: "Ok then, I'll do that and we'll meet here tomorrow at 9:00 AM"

Adam: "Splendid!"

The day was already too hectic on Adam so he went back home and started planning for The Tomorrow that will mark a beginning of an important milestone in his life and in the life of hundreds of others.

He did few calls, had interesting discussions with some of his friends and with Samantha and couple of hours later he grabbed his notebook and started writing...

Belief is the first step

Working up-side-down

Adam knew that this is the tip of the iceberg, the cutting edge of his transformation... The following 3 month would be the defining time of his life.

It was around 8 AM, when 3 people met next to the building where P Plus Inc was.

Samantha, Eddy and Adam have talked briefly on a short scenario that they will play to open the door towards Adam's New Rescue Strategy to PPlus.

Waiting for the trio, was Simone who was excited to see something new and adventurous. If Simone was into literature, she would be preparing herself to watch a Live Play of Shakespeare only this time everything is real, and the theater is the real life.

Adam started to brief everyone about what's going to happen...

At 8:30 AM they were preparing to enter the building

"And remember, no one from management should know that I'm in Charge" said Adam while holding the door to Mrs. Kays followed by Simone and Eddy.

The idea was simply to create a deceptive camouflage on the management floor by Eddy and Samantha while Adam come up with a plan enabling the actual treasure of the company to do what they do best.

"Good Morning Everyone" Said Simone to the entire board of directors who were invited all on a short notice to an urgent general meeting.

"This got to be serious" said Benjamin to Simone

Simone: "Allow me to Introduce you to Mrs. Samantha & Mr. Eddy, Delegates from The Corporate Head office"

Samantha: "Good Morning ladies & gentlemen"

Eddy: "Good Morning"

Simone: "We all know how the situation at PPlus is lately, and corporate has agreed to land a hand by sending top experts to assist you coming up with a course correction plan to the company."

Samantha: "in other words, we're here to act as both catalyst and facilitators and by working together we surely can identify the issues holding this company back and explore potential solutions... and While we're here we will also offer you some ideas that would help."

Joanna: "That sounds fantastic; I'm looking forward to that"

Samantha: "That's the spirit, what do you do Ms. _____?"

"Joanna Spring, I'm the VP of Operations and acting COO", said the elegant middle age woman while sending an almost orphan smile at both Samantha & Eddy as if she have been waiting for them for a long time.

Eddy: "Let's Start then... We will first start by representing the current situation of the company."

In the meantime, Adam was sitting with Rudy on his Desk.

Rudy: "... and that's mainly the issue, our ideas and plans and project don't get the necessary support.

We don't have budget,

We don't have Resources,

We don't even have proper access to data"

Adam: "That's horrible, but let me ask you this, what do you think is the cause of that?"

Rudy: "I believe that the main reason is that Management have been too busy with internal things that their priority list has been overflowed with urgent things that made our ideas to the bottom of the list."

Adam (thinking by himself silently): "This guy is hilarious! Even though at times like these employees try to blame it on the management irrespective if it was their fault or not... Rudy was actually giving excuses to the ignorant and reclus board of director"

Adam: "Let me ask you another question: How Confident are you that if you got Funding & the proper resources, your ideas would turn things around?"

Rudy: "I'll tell you this Adam, I have Faith in my team and that's what matters as it always had."

Adam was astonished by the spirit this young manager have. He believed in his Team, and he never separated himself from them. And at this moment it was time to say the magic word...

"I think I can HELP out" Adam said with a Proud smile on his face.

Rudy: "How will you do that? You're here since like, yesterday! And we've been here since a long time trying and failing..."

Adam: "Well didn't you hear that I was hired in like 24 hours?"

Rudy: "Yes..."

Adam: "Then I must know someone from the 15th floor who has enough influence to get me hired in such a short period of time." And he ended the sentence with a wink of his eye.

Rudy: "Right"

Adam: "So how about you let me help you here, and using my 'connection' I can make sure the Team's ideas are delivered upstairs... Properly"

Rudy had a BIG smile on his face, directly asked Faten to call on couple of members of the team for an urgent meeting.

<1 hour and a half later on the 15th floor...>

Samantha: "Wow, things are much complicated than I thought... I want to see all the numbers."

Simone looked at Cliff, the CFO of PPlus, with a strong look expecting him to start talking.

Eddy: "Mr. Cliff, your comments on this are highly appreciated."

Cliff: "ahh... well... everything is properly covered from all angles, and we've all been working hard, and I'm sure the problems we're facing are typical to any similar enterprise in this economy."

Everyone was giving him a very awkward look, so Samantha (that has already been briefed by Adam on his first impression on Cliff) calmly replied to him, in an attempt to push his limits a bit:

"In times like these, it has been statistically proven that the CFOs of the companies are the reason behind declines and bankruptcy."

Cliff: "Are you accusing me of something Madame!!???"

Samantha: "Do you want me to?"

Cliff: "You wouldn't dare!"

Samantha: "I Dare you to present the company's numbers to the board and defend yourself in the next 15 minutes?"

Cliff: "You know something... I don't have to bare this from you or anyone else... I'm leaving now and will be back when the ACTUAL CEO of the company is here not just facilitators."

And he stood up and started walking toward the door. Now the main reason for Cliff's Reaction, was simply because he was not involved properly in the Finances of the company, so obviously, he was not prepared and found the 'easy' way out.

Samantha: "Anyone else wants to join Cliff in his soon-to-be new path?"

Everyone was calm and a little bit shocked from what just happened.

Joanna & Spencer were debating who would want to comment on what just happened. So spencer, the head of marketing said:

"I don't think Cliff has anything wrong with how he performs his work, we always reviewed the numbers coming from him and they are always done properly and efficiently and whenever we sent a specific request it gets answered in an absolutely professional manner; so I think that you just made a mistake there."

Samantha: "How do you normally communicate with Cliff?"

Spencer: "via email of course and in written communication, everything is formal"

Samantha (looking at Joanna): "Do you agree with what Spencer just said?"

Joanna: "I certainly do, we never had issues with Finance or with the CFO for years. And our emails and requests are answered in a timely manner and in the most professional way possible."

Eddy: "Let us take a break for couple of hours and we'll re-join at 1 PM"

Zooming down to the 5th floor, where Rudy and key members of his team were putting together their ideas and plans.

Faten: "What do you think about this Rudy?"

Adam interrupted and said: "That's simply Awesome!"

Rudy: "I'll say with Adam, this looks great... I just hope this plan see the light."

"Leave that to me" said Adam holding his devilish smile.

Adam took all the files, sheets and presentations and headed up to the 15th floor.

Adam met privately with Samantha, Eddy and Simone and they all shared their insights and discussed for the following hour several details.

Samantha: "I'm really proud of you Adam; your plan might actually work!"

Eddy: "I'm enjoying every single moment of this!"

Simone: "Me Too! I never expected that it would be as exciting as it is right now... And we've only just begun."

Adam: "Let's not get ahead of ourselves; But after the motivation the employees have showed me down there... I would just recall this quote I heard long time ago:

'Some Goals are so worthy, it's Glorious even to Fail'

"

Eddy: "I Agree"

Samantha: "I agree on my behalf and on Dr. Kays as well."

Simone: "Who?"

Adam: "We only have some time left before the meeting gets back on, so let's go over what we will propose one more time."

Everyone was back in the large meeting room, and the meeting was rejoined.

Eddy: "Ladies and Gentlemen, Welcome back. We have one last point to cover before we move on to the suggested plans."

Simone: "We have the Numbers with us, but decoding them now would take a miracle without Cliff. Let us call on a senior person from Finance to fill in his place."

Joanna: "I don't think that is possible, we had some strict policies that were sub-optimized by department, which makes the finance department actually several small accounting departments in each division. Making the only link that would give you 360 degrees to the financial situation of the company is handled on a CFO level."

"Are you saying that if the CFO is gone, the company will collapse?" Samantha said in an ironic voice.

"Of course not, but as I told you before, everything was running smoothly so we never thought of that happening." Spencer defensively replied.

Simone: "Where's Vicky? She's the one assisting Cliff, she should be able to help."

A Voice from the room said stood up and said: "She's not available but I know someone who can help."

Everyone looked to the back of the room where the voice came from; Adam was standing holding some files in his hands.

Joanna: "And you are?"

Samantha: "Adam will be assisting us in this."

Benjamin giving the look of the person who figured everything out smiled and said in a medium loud voice:

"I knew you had some connections with Corporate."

Adam walked towards Samantha, Eddy and Simone and handed Eddy the sheets and files he was holding.

"Would you please give me just few minutes?" said Adam to everyone.

Simone: "Granted"

Adam walked out the meeting room and started walking towards the elevator.

Just before arriving there, he looked at the beautiful girl behind the reception desk.

Adam: "I never caught your name Miss _____?"

Receptionist: "Evelyn"

Adam: "Enchanté Mademoiselle" *(French for "I'm Enchanted to meet you Miss.")*

Evelyn smiled back at him while he continued talking:

"You know Evelyn, this is your lucky day! You may be minutes away from the chance you've been waiting for the past few years."

Evelyn stopped smiling, and gave Adam a weird look.

Evelyn: "I didn't catch that"

Adam: "Would you mind coming with me to the Board room?"

Evelyn: "If that's the new method in flirting, or if it's some sort of a Joke, then it isn't funny!"

Adam: "Why don't you call Vicky to fill in your place, you will be busy for the next few hours and maybe for the next months."

Evelyn: "Listen, Seriously... I'm warning you... if this is some sort of a...."

And before she could finish her sentence, Adam grabbed her hand and led her to the board room where everyone was waiting.

The board of executives had everyone looking at each other silently as the young man they met minutes ago, walking in with the receptionist in his hand;

And without any introductions, Evelyn and Adam were walking towards Simone and Samantha;

"Evelyn will be able to help out in this"
Said Adam while looking to Evelyn's
surprised face.

Samantha: "Hello young lady, we have
some sheets that needs an explanation
and you've been recommended to
assist us. Is that accurate?"

Evelyn was still in what would be
defined as a "Trance Mode",
everything around her was moving
slowly and she was too confused to
reply properly.

"Me? I don't know, that looks like a big
task and I'm just a receptionist" Said
Evelyn with a calm and scared voice.

"A Receptionist with an excellent
academic background, a functional

experience in PPlus' Finances and an un-official assistant to the CFO." Said Adam to boost her confidence and remove the suspect of everyone in the room.

Evelyn: "Well I can try" with a smile back at Adam.

Samantha gave the sheets to Evelyn who recognized everything since she was the one who actually produced them, and then Samantha started asking her some questions.

The first note Evelyn noticed, is that the sheets themselves have barely changed since she made them, which imply that the CFO and his assistant didn't do much work after her.

25 minutes later, everyone were impressed by both the level of knowledge and professionalism the young Evelyn was demonstrating in such a short notice and with such a complicated task.

Eddy: "I guess we have all the facts with us now; Ladies and gentlemen what's your overall feedback?"

The board of directors started debating some thoughts, comments and feedback on the current state of the business and in as fast as another 30 minutes; the sky was cleared from all the clouds of confusion and everyone were ready to land an action plan that would save the company.

One of the executives said in a warm and promising voice:

"I never thought how powerful a meeting with the right people and the right facilitators could bring so much output in such a short time! All we need now is a plan;"

Samantha (sending a proud smile at Adam): "and that's why we are here, we have in our possession a very good plan that we believe make a turning point to PPlus if you give it the right attention and support."

Joanna: "Let's do this!"

Samantha slipped the plan's details coming from Rudy's Team on the 7th floor and gave the floor to Adam to explain it to everyone.

An Hour passed by, and almost everyone were nodding their heads to what seemed to be crafted to the needs of the company; and they also admired the skills shown by the newest "average" employee who took the lights of the room with his confident style, selective wording and warm voice.

Spencer: "This is just what we need; you have my vote"

Samantha: "what about the rest of you? is this project worth a shot?"

Most of the hands were raised in favor of the suggested project.

Joanna: "I'll make sure all the resources needed are available; I'll also start putting together team to start the execution."

Adam: "If you don't mind, I'd like to propose someone to take the lead on this, and I'd want to act as a liaison between you and the team."

Joanna: "Your resource is internal or external?"

Adam: "I'd like to Nominate Rudy from the 7th floor and his team, they are perfect for the job."

Joanna: "Rudy and his team are hardworking employees and they have what it needs; so Yes, your suggestion is accepted."

Samantha: "I think our Job here is finished for the day; Thank you all for your time, and good luck in refreshing the company back to its golden years."

Simone: "Thank you Samantha and Eddy, I'll do the necessary administrative tasks to make sure everything is properly filed, the team is in place and the plan is ready for execution"

The day ended like magic; Samantha and Eddy left the room with a wink at Adam and Simone notifying them that an "after-party" is to be set at the end of the day.

Adam was about the leave when Evelyn stopped him and took him aside.

Evelyn:

"Are you crazy?

What were you trying to accomplish embarrassing me like this!

My heart was about to stop, I was not prepared for such a thing and I could've screw up big time"

Adam: "You're welcome. You did great in there, even better than what I was expecting"

Evelyn: "What do you expect now, a Thank you? You almost ruined my career by your foolish action"

Adam: "You call that a Career? You call yourself Ambitious? "

Evelyn: "I do, it's just that I plan things and what happened was not what I call 'Spontaneous' and I don't react well in these conditions."

Adam: "You just got yourself a promotion, and not the type of promotions that a receptionist would expect."

Evelyn: "Ok so maybe I was wrong about you in this, and I should thank you. How about I invite you out for Thank you dinner?"

Adam: "ummm... a Dinner? I donnnn't think it's a good idea"

Evelyn: "Listen I would feel much comfortable if you said yes. And please don't think of it as a Date, it's just a dinner between colleagues."

Adam didn't want to blow his cover, that's why he was trying to get out of the situation as polite as possible, but Evelyn was giving him a look that he couldn't ignore.

Adam: "Sure we could go out... But I have to warn you, I've recently got a Job and I haven't been employed for some time now... So I don't have a Dime, Your treat?"

Evelyn (smiling all over): "Yes my treat! Tomorrow evening at 8 PM"

Adam: "Deal"

Later on that evening in near coffee shop.

"You are a Genius Adam, I never expected things to turn out that well" Said Eddy while grabbing his cup of coffee.

Simone: "Well I have to give it to you, everything that was done was un-orthodox by all means, but the outcome was incredible in such a short time! You earned your reputation Adam."

Adam: "Well, I would never have done it if it wasn't for you. Thank you all of your excellent work"

Samantha: "You made me really proud today Adam, everything myself and Dr. Kays have tough you in addition to your charming experience made a great turn around."

Adam: "Thank you Mrs. K, you have no idea how much I appreciate those words coming from you... "

Simone: "So when are you planning to stop reveal your identity as the Acting Managing Director or PPlus and the next in line to be CEO?"

Adam: "What I did is based on my belief that any company has a potential of becoming great simply by placing all the ingredients in place.

And to answer your question, I'm NOT going to anytime soon.

I shall keep acting as the liaison between the board and between the employees and the plan will be executed by PPlus' Own people.

"

Simone: "I Trust you... It's your call; I shall convey what happened today to Daren & Jill;

Let's not get ahead of ourselves here but optimistically speaking if everything went based on expectation and based on the success of the transformation you will get out of the company, we'll make sure we line you up as CEO as the current one is retiring soon and he has not nominate his replacement, so if everything goes according to plan; you'll go through a period a time"

Samantha: "You will make an excellent CEO Adam. No doubts about that. I'll also make sure to be there for you coaching you all the way so you pick up to the role as soon as possible."

Playing Your Card Right

The Moment of Truth

"Team; Today, I'm speechless... I have been here long enough, and this is genuinely the first time this happens.

Not only our project got approved, but we also got a *Carte-Blanche* to use whatever resources we need to make it work" Said Rudy talking to everyone in the 7th floor.

"We need to thank our new Friend Adam, who obviously made that happen" Rudy Continued.

Faten: "Thank you Adam for your help, you've managed to make a distinguished first impression on us from your very first days."

Adam: "Rudy, Faten, Thank you for your kind words; But believe me, I'm not the person to take the credit; I was only the messenger here. I would like to give credit to your unity and spirit that made this happen; your confidence in each other and your will to make it work inspired me to land a hand and give it a try.

I had to pull some serious strength here, so TEAM LET'S DO THIS! Let's make PPlus the Company we all want it to be. I've been here for less than a week and I Love it already, YOU made me Love it...

"

Rudy: "Amen to That... You heard the guy, Team let's GO Go Go.."

Everyone started the execution immediately; Faten started putting the plan to distribute the roles and tasks, Rudy putting a list of resources and budgets to ask for... and there it was, the Spark that will define winning for PPlus and its Team.

Phase one of Mission Impossible was almost done, and Adam's mind was more occupied not by the success or failure of the overall transformation project... He was not thinking of how to break it to the Executive boards and to the employees about his real identity... and definitely not thinking of how he will look as the CEO of PPlus. He had only ONE item on his

Mind... his dinner with Evelyn tonight!

9 hours went by in 9 minutes, and everything was set in both floors, the 15th and the 7th to KickStart the Project and let the dream come true.

7:58 PM in the restaurant Evelyn chose, Adam was waiting at the table wearing his not-made-to-impress-girls uniform.

3 minutes later, Evelyn entered the restaurant wearing a genuine smile all over that made her shine across the big room full of people.

"Good Evening Evelyn" Said Adam while assisting her to sit to the table by leaving his place and pulling the chair for her.

Evelyn: "Glad you could come, Adam"

Adam was very nervous from the situation itself, although he had lots of First dates and similar situations and he's known for his unique style with girls; Only this time, it was different; Adam had a challenge of keep-saying-the-truth while not uncovering his true role.

Evelyn: "So tell me more about you, who's that mysterious guy who made an impressive first few days and managed to turn things around while being an average employee?"

Adam: "Well, let's put it this way; I have been unemployed for a while, with a past I prefer not to dig deep into now... I was referred by Simone's Manager, Daren to the Company... I didn't know what to expect, so I just followed my instincts"

Evelyn: "Well you managed yourself well, what about your presentation to the board... It was breath-taking; you grabbed all the attention of a known stubborn group; where did you learn to do that? And I'm particularly impressed by the confidence and guts you showed in there."

Adam: "You know Evelyn; I recall a time when I was at your shoe, I didn't know my full potential, and I was always thinking that my big shot will just come to me if I played by the rules long enough; and for years nothing changed.

Until there was a time where I first met the TRUE me, the young man with a dream and with the help of some dear friends, I realized that dreams doesn't come true, They either are true to begin with or they're not."

Evelyn was sitting silently admiring the words of Adam passionately as if she's listening to a symphony.

Adam: "When I saw the winner's spirit in PPlus the other day, I knew instantly that things are very close to getting better... If only the right GUT and Confidence is there to uncover the hidden truth. And there's no one better to do that but someone from the outside, who simply have nothing to lose. So I said to myself, what the heck!"

Evelyn: "and what did you see when you looked at me?"

Adam: "Evelyn, Allow me to tell you a small story

Once upon a time there where 3 birds on a tree, one of them always brought food to the nest, the other one secured the nest from external threats and the third one didn't do much but sit there all day and watch.

Every day, the 3 birds always do the same things, one brings food, one do the tour and secure the perimeter of the nest and the third one do almost nothing.

One day a Big storm came and the nest was really under a lot of pressure and it was about to get destroyed; the 3 birds got very much frightened from what would happen, and decided that the nest may not hold all of them, so one of them will have to fly out so the other 2 would be safe, and as you would guess, they were deciding that the least important bird gets chosen to leave.

The first bird suggested that it's him who bring the food so his mission is crucial for the survival of the others and without him, they would both starve to death.

The second bird gave a long talk about the external threats that might attack the next and that it's his mission to keep it safe.

Both birds looked at the third, who did nothing all the time but sit there while others did their tasks.

The third bird look at them in a sad way, and told them that his existence gave both birds a sense of purpose in their lives, and without him there was no nest to protect or to feed; Each one of them is capable to protect and feed himself, but not as a group.

So without the third bird, there would've been simply individual birds doing their thing every day.

And at the end, all 3 birds stayed on the nest and fought through the storm and kept each other's safc.

"

Evelyn: "So I'm the 3rd bird?"

Adam: "No you're not, the third bird was only a symbol, that represent the company, you see we tend to forget that a company has a personality, a spirit and a life... without that spirit, people will stop having a sense of purpose in what they are doing, and when they do, it will eventually fade and die. "

Evelyn: "and your point is?"

Adam: "you were the one that made things fall into perspective for me. Without you I wouldn't have seen it so clearly."

Evelyn: "So I'm not part of the birds? Ok as you wish... There goes the nifty talk and the happy ending"

Adam was not actually answering to Evelyn in his story but was more talking about the situation of the company as he saw it.

The company was there, "The nest", and everyone was doing their everyday tasks, "The 2 birds", when the storm hit the nest, everyone looked at the nest as an empty place with no life so they would've eventually leave and leave the nest gets destroyed. All what PPlus was missing, was the 3rd Bird, to link all of them together, that one thing that would make the company, Alive.

Although Adam was thinking in a very deep way at the moment, Evelyn was more taking things lightly and was considering the dinner as a normal get together getting to know someone new.

Evelyn: "Well again, I'd like to thank you for your push; And I wish you all the best in your career at PPlus, although I kinda think you're over-qualified to be working as a Marketing Coordinator..."

Adam: "Well, One for all and all for one, and each person's work is important."

Evelyn: "let us get divert away from business and stuff... Tell me more about you. What do you like to do in your free time, any hobbies? Do you like reading?"

There comes a time in every man's life, when he starts getting tiered of "starting over" in conversations, and where those small talks becomes a bit of a burdens than ice breakers; And even though Evelyn was both attractive and smart, and a great potential for a girlfriend, Adam didn't have that on his agenda at that time, so he only wanted to act Nice and Polite and not let his ego take control.

Adam: "I went through life the hard way, nothing was easy to me, since school all the way through college and when I started working. On both professional and personal level, I did learn the value of good friends and the value of believing in myself."

Evelyn: "well who hasn't, most of us went through life the hard way not just you Adam; I Had to pay my tuition by working part time in many places with minimum wages, and you know the story of my master's degree while working with people who didn't appreciate you and where they didn't even try to. And on a personal level, for some reason guys I've dates didn't find a great value in me becoming 'more than an receptionist' and my ambition was bigger than their affection. "

Adam could see by looking at her hidden tears that Evelyn was a person who managed to defy so many things to get where she was, and that she never gave up on her dreams despite the lack of support personally.

Adam then put his hand on top of Evelyn's Hand and looked her straight in the eyes and said to her:

"Everything is going to be all right. Trust me"

Evelyn smiled at him and they continued the light and sweet evening talking about lots of things and enjoying each other's company.

3 weeks went by, and PPlus was at the edge of transforming back to the successful company it once was.

Everyone had only one final test to do. The project would wither succeed and they would be back on track or it would fail and everybody's Job would be at stack.

It was already Monday 9:00 AM, the Alpha team was preparing to do their pitch to their golden potential customer KANATA Holding.

The big meeting room on the 15th floor was soon filled with executives;

"Mr. Wong, welcome to PPlus, it's a pleasure to have you and your team with us; Allow me to introduce you the team that will be presenting to you today." Said Spencer and continued to introduce the team that included Rudy, Faten and many others.

Adam was there in the room, but he asked explicitly that his presence be kept low profile as he oversees everything.

In the past 3 weeks Adam was un-officially coaching each of the team on different topics like creative thinking, presentation skills, business development, so they were all ready to present an excellent presentation and make a great impression.

Rudy started the meeting by giving an introduction of the objectives and the main points the pitch will include and then he gave the floor to Eduardo who indicated that each of the attendees have before them an executive summary of the numbers displayed on the screen and he continues by swapping roles between him and Faten;

All the eyes were stuck looking at the screens and the flip boards and then back to the documents before them; the room was filled with positive energy and the representatives from KANATA Holding were impressed how the pitch was engineered from many aspect to grab their attention and to answer their needs and questions even before they ask them.

2 hours later, the team was still filled with energy and actively answering the client's questions and concerns,

and every once and a while the team look at Adam sitting at the back of the Room to confirm if their behavior is up to his expectation, and only a simple node with a smile was enough to boost the confidence back at them.

Mr. Wong: "That was a very insightful presentation, I can't hide my positive impression anymore, this is exactly what we are looking for, with minor changes here and there; you might get yourself a deal there!"

Everyone was almost going to explode from happiness... but Mr. Wong added one last sentence that made everyone freeze with nothing to reply to.

"But as noticed, this project requires a big funding and I know that PPlus was having some difficulties lately, so who would give us the right guarantees that you will be able to pull it together the way you did today?"

There was silence in the room, as this was the moment of truth of the real support and confidence between the Senior Management of the Company and the Operational team.

Rudy and Faten couldn't say a word as this was not their domain; Joanna and Spencer wanted to confirm that the company will stand by its team at all time, but they for a long 8 seconds they couldn't talk until a voice came out from the end of the room.

"A4 Holding will be the main guarantor of the project; PPlus is one of our companies and we have great faith in its team, and we're willing to Bet our money on that. If they said they will do it, Stay assured that They will!" said Daren, the SVP of A4 holding, who apparently came into the room while everyone was busy with the meeting and sat next to Adam.

That was totally unexpected for the PPlus team, but little they knew that Adam was in total alignment with Daren directly or via Simone; and through the brilliance of Adam and his unbeatable style of Leadership, PPlus was receiving valuable direction from the Mother Company and from other Top executives from all the way Up to bottom.

Mr. Wong: "That's what I wanted to hcar; we shall be sending you all the paperwork to be signed by end of the week and may I congratulate you all for a Job Well Done!"

It was only the beginning of a long journey for PPlus, but the spirit that would make success happen on every level was restored thanks to the ambition and determination of the young Adam.

After the Client has left, all the team's feeling was indescribable; Rudy and Faten and the rest of the team were almost jumping of Joy and hugging each other's with congratulating words filling all the room.

Rudy: "Thank you all, it has been a Honor to being among this wonderful team. We did it! And I'd like to thank you Adam for your great contributions, I can't be more than happy to Officially welcome you to our family, I'd be more than happy to have you on my team"

Daren: "Would you all please take your seats, as I have an announcement to make."

Everyone took their seat and all the rest of the executive board were also called in to the big meeting room.

Joining the meeting for the announcement was Gavin the Current CEO of the company and Cliff the CFO.

The team was confused in how things were going on, and with Gavin whom they haven't seen for a long time and who actually was in the building but didn't assist to the meeting with KANATA Holding.

Daren: "Truth to be told, few months ago, A4's Executives did see more value in shutting PPlus' down rather than to see it operating.

Performance was not going according to expectations and in a nutshell, there was no flashing hope at the end of the tunnel for all the people working here.

We had to go through extreme negotiations with few key people within PPlus' executive team on the procedures to make it LESS painful for the team; and Gavin was on his way to an early retirement, that's what validated his long vacation."

Everyone was looking in Shock to the words of the senior executive;

"Despite our commitment to all of you, the decision of shutting PPlus' down was tough on all of us, but one of our team, Jill, suggested a talented consultant with a Revolutionary style to assist in Refreshing the Company" Continued Daren while looking in a proud smile towards Adam.

"I never thought I would say that, but I have to admit this Company needs the young spirit and the fresh leadership that Mr. Adam brought upon us to be saved and to be restored to a new era of golden years" Said Gavin.

Gavin: "Therefore I'd like to Join Daren in announcing that Adam will be next in Line for CEO of PPlus with direct support from both of us and the final transition will take place 3 months from now, and effective immediately he will be the Managing Director of PPlus reporting directly to me"

Daren: "Congratulations Adam, not only you managed to impress me, but you earned your seat leading the company toward a bright future. Well done Son!"

Simone: "Thank you all for your time; An official Memo will be sent by the end of today to all the department confirming the latest announcement; We look forward to seeing more of your leadership style flowing all over the company Adam; Congratulations again, I'm both pleased and honored to have taken part of this refresh experience."

Everyone started to leave the room and several ones were congratulating Adam for his success and his new Role.

Rudy: "Adam, I mean Sir; I really don't know what to say…"

Adam: "For now don't say a word, just call me Adam and answer me the following question."

Rudy: "Sure, which question?"

Adam: "Where do you like to have your new office?"

Rudy: "My new office?"

Adam: "When the KANATA project is done, your promotion will be waiting for you. And I'm relieving you from including the new office in the promotions' negotiation; Just make sure you don't give me hard time then."

Rudy: "I don't know what to say Sir, that's fantastic... I'm..."

Adam: "If you call me Sir one more time, I'll make sure you keep doing that for a long time... Now I've arranged with Simone for you and your team to take the rest of the day off and a small budget for you to invite them out to celebrate your achievement.

Good Job Rudy, I'm really proud to have managers like you in my team."

Rudy was almost going to cry happy tears looked with a Hard Look of Respect towards Adam and said: "Thank you Adam, you won't regret it!"

Later on at the Kays

Mrs. K: "I knew you could do it, Congratulations Adam!!"

Dr. K: "I was very happy following up on your progress, and I never doubted your abilities and I can predict a bright future with the man you have become. My respects to you Adam"

Adam: "Well, to be honest, I would've never become the person I am right now if it wasn't for both you... You are my mentors and my dear friends, and I will always owe it to you."

Mrs. K: "A mentor is like the tennis player's coach, he helps him slow down the time and sees the ball approaching Slowly for him to go and hit it... But at the end it's the player who makes it not the mentor."

Dr. K: "Indeed!"

Mrs. K: "Go and celebrate; you just made your dream come true, and that's something worth celebrating and can only be ousted by the News of FINALLY finding your Future Mrs. Adam."

Adam while he was going towards the door to start his New Life: "Thank you both for Everything. We'll stay in touch!"

A couple of hours later at a local pub, the group of friends were meeting over some drinks.

Nour: "I don't know how you did this, and frankly I don't care; Congratulations Amigo! I Wish you all the best."

Wess: "Congrats, that's wonderful news"

Eddy: "and not to forget how I played a big role in that play"

Bach: "Great news buddy, I can see that you're managing yourself well while I'm out of the country."

Adam: "I wouldn't have made it without you... Thank you for everything. Cheers for my Best Friends in this whole world"

The group of friends had a wonderful time, and Adam was soon on his way to his apartment;

Before he reached the front of his building he saw a message on his cellphone.

"You forgot to tell me the real version of the Birds story, where the 3rd bird was actually an undercover small eagle... Congratulation Boss! Eve."

Adam smiled while reading the message and continued his way to his apartment.

After taking a Long Hot shower, Adam was about to fall asleep, but decided to write one final entry on his notebook that still has few pages left.

Before he started writing, Adam started browsing through the pages, and with each page, a new set of memories gets illustrated on top of his head; The early beginnings where his ambitions were still young, all the way to different levels of his transformation, and now it was the time to conclude his notes....

2 years later...

One day at the office, Adam was having one of his regular staff meeting with his senior managers, his secretary comes in,

"I'm sorry to disturb your meeting Mr. Adam, but Dr. Kays is on your 'Always-Answer-Line' " said Sarah,

Adam: "Jason, please wrap up the last 3 points and I'll be back in a minute."

The successful Young CEO went into his office and picked up the line,

"Dr. K! How are you?"

"Yes..."

"Aha..."

"Aha..."

"Sure, I can Help you out..."

"WHAT!!!"

"YOU WANT ME TO BECOME A WAITER???"

"Now That's interesting... are you kidding... I'm definitely IN! we'll talk more this evening... Say hi to Samantha for me."

Get ready for *Work-Love Balance:*

"THE UNDERCOVER CEO"

THE END